PRINCE JUSTIN &
THE BLACK DUKE
OF THORNMOOR

Prince Justin and the Black Duke of Thornmoor

BOOK 1: The Lion Heir Series

By: R.C. Jameson

KINGDOM
— HERITAGE PRESS —

Published by
Kingdom Heritage Press

ISBN: 979-8-9959127-0-5

First Edition

This is a work of fiction. Names, characters, places, and incidents are either products of the author's imagination or used fictitiously. Any resemblance to actual persons, living or dead, events, or locales is entirely coincidental.

Printed in the United States of America

The Lion Heir Series

Book One – Prince Justin & The Black Duke of Thornmoor
Book Two – (Coming Soon)
Book Three – (Coming Soon)

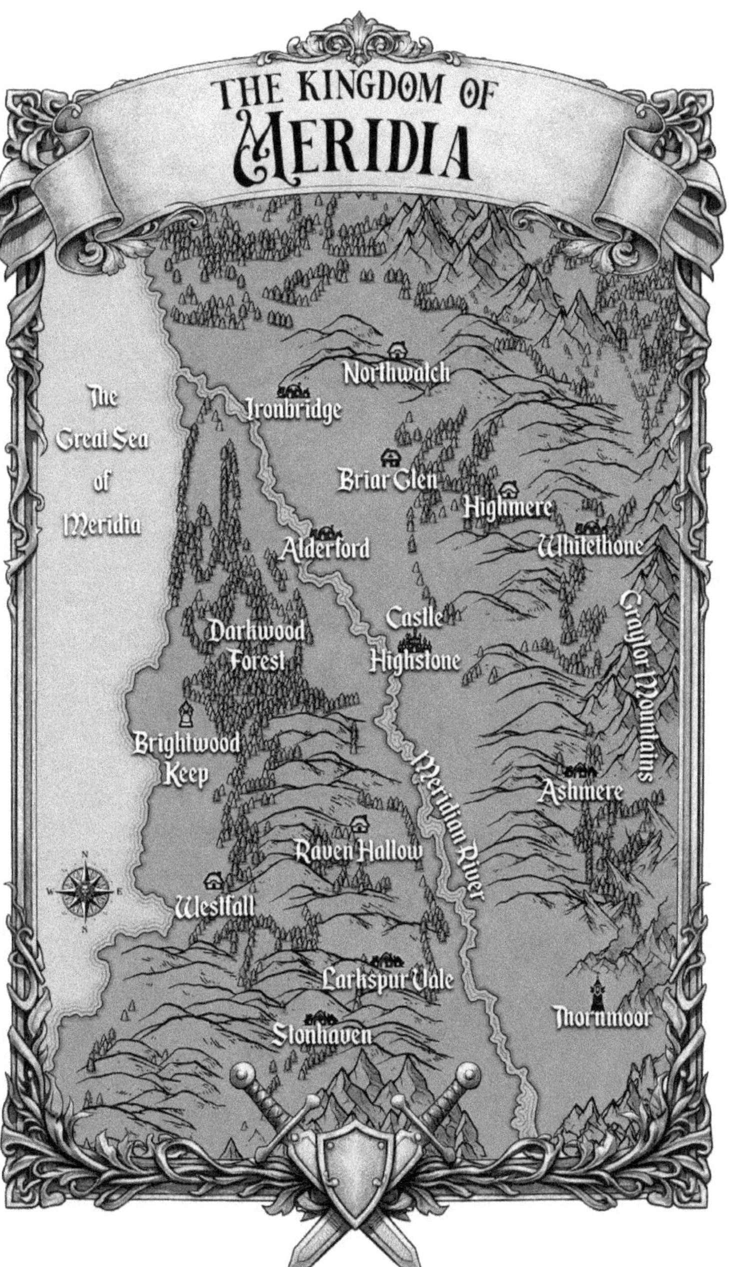

THE KINGDOM OF
MERIDIA
Northwatch
Ironbridge
The
Great Sea
of
Meridia
Briar Glen
Highmere
Whitethone
Alderford
Castle
Highstone
Darkwood
Forest
Graylor Mountains
Brightwood
Keep
Meridian River
Ashmere
Raven Hallow
Westfall
Larkspur Vale
Thornmoor
Stonhaven

Content

- Prologue -

Something moved where nothing should have been.

The sound came first. Not a roar. Not thunder. A tearing pressure in the air, like fabric stretched past its limit. The ground shuddered, and water in the well trembled as if a furnace door had swung open somewhere beyond the peaks — somewhere vast and old.

The river churned.

A woman at the well looked up toward the mountains. Her bucket sat forgotten at her feet. Her heart slammed against her ribs, too fast, a warning that came too late. The air tasted wrong. Metallic. Hot. Like standing too close to the blacksmith's forge.

The roof of the miller's house caught fire.

Not from lightning. Not from any torch. Something fell like molten rain, and the thatch burst alight while the wood beneath it blackened before it could even smoke. The heat pressed in from every direction, thinning the air, turning each breath sharp. People stumbled from their homes with hands raised against the blast, eyes streaming, throats closing on the acrid stink of burning thatch and scorched wood.

The well water hissed where droplets struck its surface.

The church steeple cracked down the center with a sound like breaking bone.

The old man saw it clearly. He would not speak of it for days, and when he finally did, his hands shook. The memory sat behind his eyes. Something that shouldn't exist. Couldn't exist. But had. Wings that did not beat but glided. A long shape folding into the smoke. Eyes that opened above the clouds, bright and terrible and aware. Twin suns burning through darkness.

A silhouette vast against the stars.

Then gone.

A father ran for the barn. The horses were trapped inside, screaming. High, piercing shrieks that cut through the roar of flames. His lungs burned with every step. His hands fumbled with the latch and blistered against hot metal. He could hear them dying. He couldn't reach them.

A mother shoved her children into the root cellar and pulled the door shut above them. Her youngest cried out, reaching back with small desperate hands. She pressed her weight against the wood, tears running down her face, whispering prayers she half-remembered. *Stay down. Stay quiet. Please, God, let them stay quiet.*

The blacksmith stood in the street, hammer raised toward the sky. His arms shook. All his strength, all his years at the anvil — useless against this. He wanted to fight. There was nothing to fight.

Someone shouted toward the river. *Get to the water!* But the river reflected the flames like a second burning sky. People ran anyway. Some made it. Some didn't. The heat came after them, scorching their backs, stealing their breath.

The air pulled inward.

Everything went still. Hearts suspended. Breath held.

Then a surge of heat flattened everything in its path. Barn walls blew outward in splinters and ash. The air caught fire, a wave of pressure and flame that rolled through the settlement like a breaking tide. Those still standing were thrown to the ground. The sound drowned out everything else.

The orchard trees bent and snapped like kindling.

The chapel bell fell silent.

It ended as fast as it had begun. No chase. No drawn-out destruction. The sky emptied, and only fire remained.

Ash fell like snow. People crawled from cellars, from the river, from behind stone walls that had somehow held. They moved through the smoke calling names. Searching. Finding some. Not finding others. Nobody spoke above a whisper. Grief was quiet that way.

Dawn came gray and cold.

Half the settlement was gone. The orchard stood blackened. The river steamed, its surface slick with soot. Survivors gathered in small clusters, hollow-eyed, silent. Some wept. Others stared at nothing. Children clung to whoever was left.

In the far distance, a thin column of smoke rose from the

upper peaks. Steady. Unmoving.

A rider mounted near the edge of the ruin. His horse stamped and shied, eyes rolling white, nostrils flaring at the smell of death. He looked back once. The people picking through ash. The shapes under blankets in the square. His jaw tightened. Someone had to carry word.

He turned south.

By the time the smoke reached Highstone, the story had already begun to change.

-v-

- Chapter I -

Morning came to Castle Highstone the way it always did.

The lion banners snapped in the wind, red and gold against gray stone. Below, in the training yard, soldiers moved through their drills in tight formation. Steel rang against steel. Boots struck packed earth in rhythm. The air smelled of cold iron and leather and the particular sharpness of a morning that hadn't decided yet whether to be kind.

From the chapel tower, bells chimed the hour, faint and steady. The sound carried across the courtyard and faded into the hills beyond.

Justin stood at the center of the yard with his sword in hand, facing his father across the packed earth. King Roland wore no crown here. Just leather training armor and a practice blade. His stance was solid, balanced. He looked less like a man who ruled a kingdom and more like one who knew how to fight.

Justin tightened his grip on the hilt. Around them, the soldiers had stopped their drills to watch from the edges of the yard. Some leaned on their spears. Others crossed their arms. None of them spoke.

He rolled his shoulders and adjusted his footing, checking his stance the way his father had taught him before every engagement. Feet shoulder-width apart. Weight centered. Blade angled to guard the body.

Roland nodded once.

Justin moved first, coming in low with a quick strike toward his father's left side. Roland deflected it easily, and the blades met with a sharp crack. Justin pulled back, circled right, and tried again, feinting high before cutting low.

Roland stepped into the strike and turned it aside.

Justin's breath came faster. He could feel the sword's heft in his hand, the strain in his wrist, the heat building under his collar despite the cold. He pressed forward with three strikes in quick succession. High. Low. Center. His father blocked each one without stepping back.

Then he saw it. An opening. Roland's guard had shifted slightly left, just enough to exploit. He committed to a hard diagonal cut, angled to slip past his father's blade and tap his shoulder. A clean move. Textbook. The kind of strike that ended sparring matches.

Roland didn't block it. He sidestepped.

He'd known. The moment Justin committed, he'd known.

Justin's momentum carried him forward, too far, and his balance tipped. He tried to recover, but his father's blade was already there. A light tap against Justin's wrist. Not hard. Just enough.

Justin's sword clattered to the ground.

The yard went quiet.

Roland lowered his blade. He wasn't smiling, but his expression carried a patience that made the moment heavier than any rebuke. "You overcommitted," he said. His voice was steady, measured, and it cut through the silence of the yard the way a chisel cuts stone. Clean and without apology.

Justin's face burned. He bent to retrieve his sword, keeping his eyes on the dirt.

"You saw the opening," Roland continued. His tone wasn't harsh or disappointed, just instructional, as if this were another lesson. "But you didn't confirm it. An enemy will bait you with false weakness. You have to know the difference."

Justin nodded. His throat felt tight as he gripped the hilt of his recovered sword.

"You fought well," his father added, and something genuine came through in his voice. "Your form is strong. Your strikes are clean. But strength without patience leaves you exposed."

Around them, a few soldiers murmured their approval. One clapped briefly. Another nodded. Gestures of respect meant to soften the blow. Justin heard the praise and registered it somewhere in the back of his mind, but all he could think about was the sword in the dirt. The mistake. His father correcting him in front of everyone who mattered.

He straightened and sheathed his blade, forcing his hands to stay steady, his face to stay calm. He'd learned how to do that. How to look composed even when something twisted and coiled inside his chest.

Roland raised an eyebrow. That gaze of his always saw too

much. "Ready to try that again, or do you need a moment?"

Justin shook his head. "I'm done for today, Father."

Roland studied him for a long moment, expression unreadable, then placed his hand on Justin's shoulder. Firm. Warm. Somehow both comforting and unbearable. "You'll get it," he said quietly, low enough for Justin's ears alone. "You're learning."

Justin nodded again. He didn't trust himself to speak.

His father turned and walked toward the soldiers, calling out instructions for the next drill. The men moved back into formation. The yard filled with noise again. Boots and steel and the crack of wood practice shields. Justin stood alone in the center, looking down at his hands. They weren't shaking. That was good, at least.

But he'd still failed. Not badly. Not in a way that mattered to anyone else. He knew the truth of it, though. He'd seen the opening and lunged too quickly. Impatient. Reckless. His father had been right to correct him.

Justin exhaled slowly and turned toward the edge of the yard.

That's when he saw her.

Lady Elayne stood on the balcony overlooking the courtyard, pale blue dress, dark hair pulled back in a simple braid. His stomach dropped. She wasn't watching the soldiers. She was watching him.

Their eyes met. Everything sharpened. She'd seen all of it.

The mistake. His father's correction. The flush in his cheeks, the way he'd stood there unable to speak. She didn't smile or wave. Just watched him with that quiet, steady gaze she always had. The one that made him feel like she saw more than she said.

Especially not now. Not after this.

Justin looked away first. He hated himself for it even as he did it.

He walked toward the armory, his stride measured and controlled. He didn't glance back at the balcony, though he could still feel her eyes on him.

Behind him, his father's voice rose above the clatter of the yard, calling out a name that made Justin stop mid-stride.

"Lawrence!"

Justin turned just enough to see his younger brother sprinting across the courtyard, tunic half-untucked, hair wild, grinning the way only an eight-year-old could.

"Father!" Lawrence shouted as he ran. "I found a nest in the stables! Three baby sparrows! Can I keep one?"

Roland laughed. A real laugh, deep and warm — the kind Justin couldn't remember hearing directed at him in months. Maybe years.

"You can't keep a sparrow, son," Roland said, and even his refusal carried a gentleness that made Justin's chest tighten. "They're meant to fly."

"But what if it doesn't want to fly yet?"

"Then you wait until it's ready."

Lawrence threw his arms around their father's waist. Roland ruffled his hair with an easy affection that came without thought or effort, still smiling as if nothing in the world mattered more than this moment with his youngest son. For a breath, his father's face softened in a way Justin rarely saw anymore — the same expression he used to wear when Mother was still alive.

Justin watched them. The contrast settled over him like something he'd grown used to carrying. His father's voice was different with Lawrence. Lighter. Unburdened by expectation. No talk of openings or patience or what it meant to fail in front of soldiers who would one day follow you into battle.

When had he last heard that laugh?

Justin turned and kept walking. His jaw was tight. His eyes stayed fixed on the armory ahead. He didn't blame Lawrence. His brother was eight, still young enough to be a child without consequence. Still free from the crown's weight that Justin had been born beneath. Lawrence could chase sparrows and laugh without thinking about what it meant. Could throw his arms around their father without wondering if he'd done something wrong that day.

Justin couldn't. He'd long since stopped wishing otherwise.

He climbed the stone steps to the battlements, where the wind was stronger. It tugged at his cloak and stung his face as he walked to the edge and looked out over the kingdom.

Highstone sat on a hill overlooking the valley. Below, the fields stretched green and gold in the morning light, villages dotting the landscape, roads winding between them like threads. To the west, the forest rose dark and thick past the river. To the east, from south to north, ran the Graylor Mountains. Jagged peaks, gray stone, shadows that never quite lifted.

Justin stared at them.

Somewhere in those mountains, something was burning.

He could see it now. A thin column of smoke rising from the foothills. Barely visible. Just a smudge against the sky. It had been there for days, and the wind brought nothing with it. No smell of pine char or dry wood. Just cold mountain air and the kind of stillness that felt deliberate.

His father said it was a wildfire. Natural. Nothing to worry about.

Justin wasn't sure.

The smoke didn't move like wildfire. It rose straight and steady, as if from a single source. And the reports from the northern villages had been strange. Burned fields. Livestock gone. Travelers who swore they'd heard something in the mountains at night. Something that wasn't wind.

Justin gripped the stone wall. He thought about the sparring match. The mistake. The correction. His father's voice when he spoke to Lawrence. The way Lady Elayne had looked at him from the balcony. The smoke in the north.

One day, all of this would be his. The kingdom. The soldiers. The decisions. And he had to be ready.

The wind picked up. The lion banners snapped louder. But Justin didn't move. He stood on the battlements and watched the smoke rise from the mountains, wondering if strength was something you were born with or something you had to prove.

-9-

- Chapter II -

The council chamber was warmer than the battlements, but Justin felt no relief in it. Stone walls rose around him, carved with lions and crowned shields, tapestries hanging stiff between the narrow windows. Old kings, old battles, old victories, all of them watching. The long oak table ran the length of the room, its surface darkened over centuries to the color of dried blood, catching light from high windows in dull amber strips. The air smelled of candle wax and cold stone and the faint leather of Malric's armor already in his chair at the far end.

His father sat at the head, flanked by his advisors: Captain Aldric, Lord Brennan the Master of Coin, Lady Maren who governed the eastern provinces. Justin had been placed at the far end, across from his father, as far from the center of the room as the table allowed. Duke Malric of Thornmoor occupied the seat to Roland's left, the place of honor, and whether he had earned it or simply claimed it was a question Justin had never been able to answer to his own satisfaction. The other councilors deferred to the king, as they should. But they noticed when Malric spoke. They leaned forward when he gestured. His words carried a gravity that didn't require a crown.

Malric's armor was dark iron and leather, not black but close, functional and severe in a way that matched the lean angles of his face and his close-trimmed beard. His eyes were gray and steady. His hair was jet black, silver-streaked at the temples, and it lent him something between distinction and danger. He didn't look cruel. He looked certain, and in that certainty lived a kind of power that pressed against the walls of the room.

Roland stood, and the chamber went quiet.

Justin dropped his gaze to the table. The oak grain ran in long slow waves beneath his hands, cold and faintly rough where age had lifted the polish, and he pressed his palm flat against it as the prayer and the council and the smoke in the north all bore down on him at once.

"Father in Heaven," Roland said, his voice clear and unhurried, "we ask for wisdom in this hour. That we might govern justly. That we might protect the weak and uphold the right. Guide our words and our choices, that they may honor You and serve Your people. In Christ's name, amen."

"Amen," the council echoed.

Justin said it too. The word was familiar in his mouth, worn smooth by years of use, and yet this morning it caught somewhere between habit and question. He glanced up. His father's face was calm, eyes closed a moment longer than protocol required, genuine in a way that couldn't quite be faked. Malric had bowed his head with the others, but his expression gave nothing away: not mockery, not reverence. Just stillness, the way a man looks at something he acknowledges but does not need. The sight settled something uncomfortable in Justin's chest, a question he didn't want to ask himself about where faith ended and performance began.

Roland sat and nodded to Captain Aldric, who smoothed a map across the table with weathered, faintly trembling hands. The northern provinces, the Graylor passes, the foothills climbing toward the mountains.

"Three villages have sent word in the past week," Aldric said, his voice steady. "Burned fields near the passes, livestock missing. Two families from the outer farms have disappeared entirely. No bodies. No signs of struggle."

Lord Brennan leaned forward. "Bandits?"

"The villagers think so." Aldric's tone carried its own quiet dissent. "But the burns are strange, too hot and too complete. And the timing: all of it within a fortnight."

Lady Maren frowned. Her fingers drummed once against the table, a single sharp knock. "Have the patrols seen anything?"

"Nothing confirmed," Aldric admitted. "But the men are uneasy. They say the air smells wrong near the passes. Like sulfur."

Justin's chest tightened. The smoke. That thin, steady column rising from the foothills, visible from the battlements just that morning — he'd told himself it was nothing.

"Sulfur," Roland repeated, leaning back with his fingers steepled. "That could mean many things. A hot spring. A coal vein burning underground."

"Or something else," Malric said.

His voice was quiet. But something in the room shifted, not in any way Justin could point to, only that the light from the windows seemed fractionally less warm, and the silence around Malric's words lasted a beat too long.

"The people are afraid," Malric continued, measured and reasonable, his tone the kind that invites agreement without demanding it. "Fear spreads faster than fire. If we don't act decisively, the northern provinces will lose faith in the crown's ability to protect them."

Roland nodded slowly. "I agree we must act. The question is how."

He looked around the table. Justin noticed, for the first time, the faint lines beneath his father's eyes. The way his shoulders carried something that had nothing to do with his armor. When had that appeared? Or had it always been there, and Justin simply hadn't looked?

"I propose grain relief to the affected villages," Roland said. "Double the patrols along the passes, quietly, no banners, no declarations. We investigate carefully. We don't escalate until we know what we face."

Lord Brennan nodded. Lady Maren murmured her approval. Justin watched his father, studying the measured response that made perfect sense and yet left something restless turning in him.

Malric leaned forward. Slow. Deliberate. The leather of his armor creaked softly in the quiet.

"With respect, Your Majesty," he said, "hesitation emboldens enemies."

Roland met his gaze. "And recklessness creates them."

Malric didn't flinch.

"I would never speak of recklessness," he said, "not when the stakes are so high and the people look to you for guidance in their darkest hour. I speak only of clarity, of giving our people what they need. Not just grain, though that is generous and good. Something more sustaining than bread alone. They need to see the strength that has always defined this kingdom, to know in their bones that their king won't stand idle while his lands burn and his people suffer."

"And what would you have me do?" Roland asked, patient, unguarded.

"Send a full garrison to the northern passes," Malric said, leaning back slightly to show he was offering counsel rather than pressing an agenda. "Fortify the villages so that mothers can sleep without fear and children can play without looking over their shoulders. Make it known through action, not proclamation, that any threat to Meridian soil will be met with overwhelming force. Show the people, and more importantly whoever is responsible, that this kingdom doesn't wait to be struck before it rises to defend itself."

Justin's pulse quickened. Something in Malric's voice caught hold of him, not anger, not cruelty, but a kind of unwavering certainty that cut through all the confusion that had plagued him since dawn on the battlements.

"Fear is a tool," Malric continued, his words moving with the ease of simple truth. "It can be wielded by bandits and raiders, or it can be wielded by kings. If we don't claim it first, someone else will."

The logic of it settled over Justin like a hand pressing down on his shoulder. He hadn't known he was waiting for it.

Roland rubbed his jaw. He was quiet a moment, and Justin noticed again how the lines at the corners of his father's eyes had deepened in the past year, carved deeper since Mother died, since the crown stopped being shared. When Roland spoke, his voice was gentle.

"The Lord has not given us a spirit of fear," he said, "but of power, and of love, and of a sound mind."

Something flickered in Malric's eyes. Not dismissal, but a patient tolerance that made Justin wonder, just for a moment, whether his father's words sounded as uncertain to everyone else as they suddenly did to him.

"Scripture is a guide, Your Majesty," Malric said, his tone respectful, unmoved. "But it doesn't patrol borders."

He didn't have an answer. He wasn't sure his father did either.

Justin's breath caught. He waited for Roland's response with something uncomfortably close to doubt, unsettled by the possibility that the old certainties had finally been laid against something they couldn't match — and come up short.

No one spoke.

Roland's face remained calm, but his eyes held something deeper. A quiet sorrow, perhaps, or the settled resignation of a man who had heard this argument before and knew its shape. "You're right," he said, each word chosen with deliberate care. "Scripture doesn't patrol borders. Men do. And men must choose what kind of kingdom they'll defend, one built on fear, or one built on justice."

"Justice without strength is only sentiment, Your Majesty," Malric said.

Justin leaned forward slightly, drawn by the clarity of it.

"And strength without justice is only tyranny," Roland replied.

The words hung between them. Neither man reached for them. Neither man stepped back.

Justin looked from his father's face, steady and resolute, tempered by something gentler he couldn't quite name, to Malric's, which was just as unwavering but sharper, honed to a single purpose. Neither looked away. And Justin admired it, against his better instincts. The willingness to hold ground against a king.

"I'm not proposing tyranny," Malric said quietly. "I'm proposing survival. The north is burning, the people are afraid, and if we don't act with certainty, we'll lose them. Not to bandits, but to doubt."

He turned his head.

His gray eyes found Justin and held there, with an intensity that made the prince feel suddenly visible in a way his father's careful glances never quite achieved.

"A king must be many things," Malric said, still holding his gaze. "But above all, he must be sure."

Sure. The word landed somewhere below Justin's ribs.

He'd felt the lack of it on the battlements, in the training yard, in the quiet before sleep when the day's decisions replayed themselves and he picked them apart, wondering what a better prince would have done instead. His father had certainty too, but a different kind: quieter, rooted in something Justin couldn't always see, willing to wait when every instinct said to move. Malric's certainty was another thing entirely. It didn't hesitate. It didn't look back. It didn't seem to cost anything at all.

Roland exhaled slowly, the responsibility of the moment settling across his shoulders. "I hear your counsel, Duke Malric," he said, "and I don't dismiss it lightly. But I won't send soldiers into the north without knowing what we truly face. Fear isn't a foundation. It's a fire, and fire consumes everything it touches."

He looked around the table, meeting each councilor in turn.

"We'll send relief to those who need it. We'll increase patrols along the northern roads and investigate carefully what's happening in those villages. If there's a threat, we'll meet it with the full strength of this kingdom. But we won't become the thing we fight in the process."

Lady Maren nodded. Lord Brennan murmured his assent from across the table.

Malric said nothing. He leaned back in his chair, expression carefully composed, eyes staying on Justin even as the king continued speaking. No protest in his silence. Something more patient than protest.

Roland stood. The scrape of his chair against stone cut

through the room. "That's my judgment," he said. "Captain Aldric, see to the arrangements. We'll convene again in three days to assess our progress."

The council rose. Justin rose with them, feeling the stiffness in his legs from sitting so long in tension, the cold of the stone floor pressing up through his boots. The others filed out through the heavy doors, voices fading into the corridor beyond, while Roland gathered the maps from the table with slow, deliberate movements.

Justin turned to leave, already thinking of the training yard and the familiar rhythm of steel on steel, when a voice stopped him at the threshold.

"Your Highness."

He turned. Malric stood at the far end of the table, alone now that the others had gone, his posture relaxed, his attention fixed entirely on Justin. The candles along the wall caught the edge of his dark armor, throwing long shadows across the carved stone. The room smelled of old wax and cold air and the faint must of tapestries that had never quite dried.

Justin hesitated for only a beat, then walked back, the stone floor cold through the soles of his boots.

"You fought well this morning," Malric said, and there was genuine approval in it, the kind of recognition Justin had been hungry for without knowing it until now.

Justin blinked. "You saw?"

"I make it my business to see most things that matter." Malric's glance moved briefly to the maps still scattered across the table, then returned. "Tell me. How long do you think it will take for grain to reach the northern villages, traveling by the routes your father's council approved?"

Justin worked it through. "A week. Perhaps more, if the roads are as damaged as the reports suggest."

"And the families that have already disappeared?" Malric asked, his tone steady, almost gentle, less a challenge than a man helping another work through a problem.

He didn't have an answer. Malric already knew that.

The silence between them pressed against Justin's chest, full of implications he could feel without naming them.

Malric's gray eyes held his. Not accusation in them, but something more complex: the look of a man who believes they are both grappling with a truth that good men sometimes cannot bring themselves to see. "Your father is a good man," Malric said quietly, and in those five words Justin heard both genuine respect and the faint outline of a limit. "But there will come a time when you must make a hard choice, between doing what feels right and doing what will actually save lives. When that moment comes, what will you wish you had learned sooner?"

He stepped closer. The candlelight shifted with him, shadows moving across the planes of his face.

"Do you know yet what you would choose?"

Justin's pulse hammered in his ears. He wanted to answer, to prove he understood what Malric was asking. But the words tangled. He wasn't sure whether the answer Malric wanted was the one his father would give, and the space between those two possibilities felt like ground falling away underfoot.

Malric studied him a moment longer. Justin had the sense that the older man could read every question written on his face, the desire to be worthy and the fear that worthiness might require him to become something his father wouldn't recognize. Then something shifted in Malric's expression, settling toward what might have been satisfaction. He turned toward the door with the easy confidence of a man who has planted a seed and intends to let it grow.

Justin stood alone.

The tapestries hung still on the walls. The stone lions watched from their carved ledges, indifferent to everything beneath them. The oak table stretched before him, empty now except for scattered maps and the dark rings left by cups no one had bothered to clear, and through the narrow windows the smoke was still rising from the north. He wondered if his father was right to move with such caution, or if Malric understood something essential that Roland's goodness prevented him from seeing, or if the truth was something neither of them had named yet. Something Justin would one day be forced to find on his own, when the choice was his alone and the consequences fell on no one else's shoulders. The smoke rose and kept rising, thin and patient, like a question no one had answered yet.

- **Chapter III** -

Malric paused at the doorway. He didn't turn.

His silhouette held still against the dim corridor light, and the smell of cold stone and old iron drifted back through the doorway: the smell of a man who spent more time in armor than in halls.

"Your Highness," he said. Not a command, exactly. Not a request either. "Walk with me."

Justin followed.

The corridor stretched ahead of them in silence, stone walls cut by narrow windows that let in the pale afternoon light. Somewhere deep in the keep, a bell was finishing its toll, one slow note dissolving into quiet. Their footsteps moved out of rhythm with each other, Malric's boots striking the stone in steady, unhurried beats, Justin's quicker and less certain.

Malric stopped at a window overlooking the northern hills, his gaze fixed on the horizon.

"Tell me," he said. "What did you see this morning when you looked out from the battlements?"

Justin hesitated. The corridor air pressed cool against his neck. *Nobody knew. He'd gone alone, before the council had even convened, before the castle had fully woken around him.*

"Smoke," he said, at last.

"And what did it mean to you?"

The question settled between them. Justin thought of the council table, his father's measured voice, the careful calculations and grain shipments that would take a week to arrive.

"It meant something was wrong."

Malric nodded slowly. Not satisfied, not dissatisfied. "And what will you do about it?"

"I'm not king yet."

"No." Malric turned to face him, his expression neither harsh nor gentle. "But you will be. When that day comes, will you know what to do, or will you still be wondering what it all means?"

Justin's jaw tightened. "My father—"

"Your father is a good man." The words weren't dismissive. They were simply stated, the way you'd state a fact that required nothing more. "But goodness and governance aren't the same thing. One is a virtue, the other is a skill."

He gestured toward the northern hills, his hand sweeping across the landscape beyond the glass.

"How many villages lie beyond those passes?"

"Seven?" Justin said. "Maybe eight."

"And how many families have disappeared?"

Silence.

Justin had no answer. The quiet stretched between them like a crack in the floor you couldn't stop looking at.

"You don't know," Malric said quietly. "Neither does your father. Neither does anyone sitting at that table debating grain shipments and patrol routes as if arithmetic and governing were the same thing."

He stepped closer. Leather and iron and the faint sharpness of the corridor's cold air.

"Do you understand what that means?"

Justin's throat felt tight. "It means we need better scouts."

"It means," Malric said, letting the words settle before he continued, "we are governing from a distance, making decisions on reports and assumptions and hope rather than knowledge."

He let the last word stand alone a moment.

"Hope isn't a strategy, Your Highness."

Justin wanted to argue. He wanted to defend his father, defend the patience and wisdom he'd been taught, defend all the careful deliberation that had always felt, to him, like strength. But the words wouldn't come. *Part of him already believed it.* Some small, cold part he'd rather not have acknowledged had been nodding along from the first question.

Malric watched him for a moment longer. Something in that gaze made Justin feel younger than he was, more exposed than he wanted to be. Then the duke turned back toward the window with an ease that suggested he'd moved past the conversation in his own mind already.

"I'd like to extend an invitation," he said, so smoothly that Justin took a moment to register what was being offered. "Come to Thornmoor with me. See how governance works when it's stripped of illusion, when decisions aren't softened by distance or cushioned by hope."

Justin's pulse quickened. "Thornmoor?"

"A fortnight, perhaps less if you find the education insufficient." Malric's tone stayed measured, almost gentle, but underneath it something else moved, the way a hand extended over dark water has a different quality than a hand extended over dry ground. "Your father has taught you virtue, and that is good, necessary, even. But a king must understand more than virtue if he's going to survive what's coming. He must understand power not as councils describe it but as it actually exists."

"My father wouldn't—"

"Your father," Malric said, with a softness that made the words more absolute, not less, "won't forbid it. He knows you must learn. He knows you must see the world as it is, not as we wish it to be, and he trusts that I can show you things Highstone cannot." He paused. The silence felt deliberate, measured to the syllable. "The question is whether you're ready to see them. Whether you're willing to step outside these walls and learn what it means to rule without your father's shadow to fall back on."

The words settled over Justin like a cloak he hadn't asked to wear.

"What would I see?" he asked. The question came out smaller than he'd intended.

"Order," Malric said, with the simplicity of someone describing weather. "Discipline. A people who know their place and don't question it. A land where decisions are made swiftly and carried out without the hesitation that turns resolve into regret." He turned to face Justin again, and there was something in the movement that suggested Justin's answer was already accounted for, already folded into whatever calculations the Duke of Thornmoor had made before this conversation began. "You'd see what happens when a ruler doesn't wait for councils to debate endlessly. When he doesn't hope that grain will arrive in time, or that prayers will be enough. When he simply acts because action is what the moment demands."

Justin's hands clenched at his sides, fingers pressing into his palms. "And if I refuse?"

"Then you refuse." Malric's expression didn't change. The ease of it was almost worse than a threat. "But one day you'll stand where your father stands, and you'll face a choice that won't wait for contemplation. You'll wonder if you understood enough to make it, whether you'd seen enough of the world to know what was required."

He stepped past Justin toward the corridor, unhurried, a man with other matters already waiting.

"Think on it, Your Highness. Or don't. I leave for Thorn-moor in three days regardless. If you wish to come, send word."

Then he was gone, his footsteps fading down the corridor in that steady, unvarying rhythm: the sound of a man who had never once doubted where he was going.

Justin stood at the window alone. The smoke on the northern hills had thinned, but it was still there: a faint gray line drawn against the sky like a question no one had answered yet. He thought of his father's voice in the council chamber, steady and faithful and measured. Then he thought of Malric's questions, still hanging in the air where the man himself had stood.

He wondered which of them was right.

The chapel bell rang for evening prayer.

Justin crossed the courtyard as the air turned cool around him, the shadows stretching long and thin across the paving stones. The guards nodded as he passed. He turned the corner near the fountain and stopped.

The sound of water reached him before he saw her. A soft, continuous murmur against the stone basin, threading through the quiet of the evening. Lady Elayne of Briar Glen sat on the fountain's edge, trailing her fingers through the water. Her dark hair was pulled back in a simple braid, and the green dress she wore was practical, not ornate, the hem just above the wet stone. She hadn't noticed him.

He could have turned back. There was another path. But the moment he slowed, turning back became obvious, so he continued forward.

Elayne looked up. Her gray eyes widened slightly, and she rose quickly, smoothing her skirt in one practiced motion. It was the kind of gesture that made Justin suddenly aware of his own hands, which he realized he had no idea what to do with.

"Your Highness," she said, her voice careful and formal in a way that made the space between them feel wider than the few feet it actually was.

"Lady Elayne." He stopped a few paces away. Not close enough to sit beside her, not far enough to seem rude, though he couldn't have explained why the distance mattered or why his chest felt tight.

An awkward silence opened between them. The fountain kept its murmur. The evening air carried the smell of damp stone and somewhere, faintly, the green sharpness of the garden beyond the wall.

"I was just..." Elayne gestured vaguely at the fountain. In the evening light her hands were pale, slender. "The evening is pleasant."

"It is," Justin said, and immediately felt like an idiot.

Another silence, heavier than the first. Heat crept up the back of his neck.

"You were in council today," she said. Not quite a question, but he felt grateful for something concrete to hold onto.

"Yes."

"My father received word this morning about the north." She paused, choosing her words with that careful deliberateness she always brought when speaking to him. "Burned fields. Families missing."

Justin nodded. He should have said something more. The words were there, somewhere, but reaching them felt harder than it should.

"It must be concerning," Elayne continued, her voice softer now. "For the kingdom."

"It is."

She looked back toward the fountain, her hands clasping in front of her now, formal and guarded, retreating into some safer version of herself.

"Your father will know what to do," she said quietly. There was something almost reassuring in her certainty. She believed it completely. He could tell. "He always does."

Something tightened in Justin's chest. The words came out before he could stop them. "Does he?"

Elayne glanced at him, surprise moving across her face.

"I only meant—"

"I know what you meant," Justin said. Even as he spoke he could hear the edge in his voice, too quick, too defensive.

He watched her flinch at it.

The silence that followed was worse than all the others. Justin forced himself to soften, though the damage was already done. "Forgive me. I didn't sleep well."

"Of course, Your Highness." She turned back to the fountain, her posture stiff now, the careful distance between them feeling like something he'd carved himself. "I should go. The chapel bell..."

"Yes," Justin said, taking the excuse she'd offered. "Prayer."

They stood there a moment longer, neither quite moving. Everything he should say pressed against his throat and found no way out.

"I'll walk that way," Elayne said, her voice carefully neutral. "If you're going to the great hall."

"Very well."

They set off across the courtyard together. The evening light slanted through the high windows in long golden bars, and the stone walls glowed warmer than the air actually was. The guards stood at their posts with the same steady vigilance they'd kept for years. The castle felt solid, unchanging, exactly what it had always been.

But Justin was acutely aware of her beside him. Aware of the space between them that felt both necessary and wrong. Aware of the formality hanging in the air between them like something fragile, waiting to be broken. Aware of all the things neither of them knew how to say, and probably never would.

At the great hall entrance, Elayne paused. He hated that he noticed the way she hesitated. Hated that some part of him wanted her to stay, even though he had no right to want anything from her at all.

"Your Highness," she said. "Whatever is troubling you, I hope it resolves well."

He looked at her. For a moment he almost said it. All of it: Malric and the invitation that felt more like a test, the questions that had followed him out of the corridor, the grief still lodged somewhere beneath his ribs after losing his mother, the doubts that gnawed at him in the dark. The impulse rose and fell in the space of a breath. Because she was a stranger, really. A noble girl from Briar Glen he'd barely spoken to before today. Not a confidant. Not someone who should matter to him at all.

"Thank you, Lady Elayne," he said. The words felt inadequate and final at once.

She nodded and turned toward the chapel. Justin watched her go, and the sense of loss that moved through him made no sense whatsoever. It irritated him even as he felt it, because she was nothing to him and he was nothing to her and this foolish melancholy had no business existing.

He entered the great hall alone. The emptiness of it held its silence.

Still, as he climbed the stairs to his chamber, he thought of her. The awkwardness between them. The moment when she'd sensed something was wrong and hadn't known how to help. The distance she'd maintained. Not coldly. She understood the rules as well as he did and was trying, carefully, to follow them.

It unsettled him in a way he couldn't name.

That night, Justin lay awake listening to the fire burn low.

The room darkened by degrees until only the embers remained, throwing a faint red glow across the hearthstone. Wood smoke drifted warm and thick near the fire; beyond its reach the air went cold, and he could feel the chill at the edge of his blanket where the warmth didn't quite extend. Outside, wind moved through the trees with a sound like distant water.

He thought of his father's voice in the council chamber: *We do not act in haste.* And of Malric's questions, which had followed him out of the corridor like a second shadow: *Do you know yet?*

He thought of the smoke rising from the north. Of the families that had disappeared. Of the grain shipments still a week away.

And he thought of Elayne's voice, the quiet certainty in it: *Your father will know what to do.* Said with such quiet confidence. Patience and virtue, always enough.

She belonged to his father's world. To Highstone. To the careful restraint and measured deliberation that had always defined everything Justin had been raised to believe.

And yet she unsettled him.

Not because she was wrong. Because she reminded him of everything his father believed, and everything Malric said wasn't enough.

Justin sat up, crossed to the desk, and lit the candle. His hands moved steadily. The rest of him did not.

A king had to understand virtue. His father had taught him that, and it was true, and Elayne embodied it: the restraint, the faith, the careful adherence to what was right. But a king also had to understand power. If Malric could teach him that, if Thornmoor could show him what his father's court could not, then wasn't it his duty to go? Not because he doubted his father. Because a king had to see every model, understand every approach, be prepared for the moment when virtue alone wasn't enough.

He thought of Elayne, and the chapel she'd been walking toward, and the prayer she would offer for whatever troubled him.

He thought of Malric, and the certainty in his voice, and the invitation to see the world as it was.

Two directions. Two worlds.

He couldn't stay suspended between them forever.

Justin took a piece of parchment and dipped the quill. The scratch of it against the page cut through the quiet like something small and irreversible.

He didn't let himself think about it. Just wrote.

Duke Malric,

I accept your invitation. I will accompany you to Thornmoor.

Prince Justin of Highstone

He sealed the letter with wax and set it on the desk.

Then he returned to bed. The fire had burned to almost nothing, a low glow that barely touched the ceiling. The wind moved through the trees outside, steady and indifferent. Justin lay still in the dark, staring up at nothing, and wondered if he had just made the right choice, or his first mistake.

- **Chapter IV** -

The study was cold that morning. Not the sharp, biting cold
of the night, but the slow chill that settles into stone rooms
before a fire is lit, and Roland hadn't lit one. He stood at
the window above the courtyard, his back to the door, and
Justin waited in the doorway with the smell of extinguished
candles hanging in the air and the distant clatter of a cart
crossing the cobblestones below.

He had been summoned an hour ago. No explanation, only
a page at his chamber door with a quiet message: *The king
requests your presence.* Now Roland stood holding a piece of
parchment in one hand, the broken seal swinging from its
edge, and Justin knew it before he could read a single word.

Of course. Of course he already knew.

"When were you planning to tell me?" Roland asked. His
voice was measured. Controlled.

Justin stepped into the room. "I was going to speak with you
today."

"After the letter had already been sent," Roland said, and
this time there was no mistaking the tightness in his jaw, the
way his fingers pressed the parchment as though he might
crumple it. "After Malric extended an invitation to my son,
to the heir of Highstone, without so much as a word to me.
And after you accepted it the same way."

Justin said nothing. Any defense he offered now would sound like an excuse, and they both knew it.

Roland turned from the window. For a moment the anger was there in his eyes, bright and sharp, but then something shifted, something gave way beneath it, and what remained was harder to look at than rage.

"You accepted an invitation to Thornmoor, to stay as Duke Malric's guest, without consulting me first," Roland said. The edge had left his voice.

"Yes, sir."

"Why?" The question hung between them. Roland's hand loosened on the parchment, the tension draining from his shoulders as though he'd been holding himself upright through will alone.

Justin met his father's gaze and found something he hadn't expected: not just disappointment, but a grief that sat behind his eyes and made Justin's chest go tight. "Because I knew what you would say."

"And what would I have said?" No challenge in the words. A genuine question.

"That it wasn't necessary. That I could learn what I needed here. That Malric's methods aren't—" Justin paused. "That they aren't ours."

"And you disagree." Not quite a question.

"A king needs to understand all models of governance." Justin kept his voice steady even as his father's expression grew distant. "You taught me that. If I'm to rule one day, I need to see how other lords maintain order, how they protect their people, even if their methods differ from ours."

Roland was quiet. In the silence Justin could see him wrestling with something that had nothing to do with Malric or Thornmoor or governance at all.

A narrator who has watched fathers and sons long enough might recognize what it was: Roland wasn't angry at the letter. He was afraid for the boy.

Then Roland crossed to the desk and set the letter down with a deliberateness that made Justin's pulse lift, as though the small gesture carried a weight out of all proportion to itself.

"Thornmoor is not Highstone," he said. "What Malric will show you, what he will teach you, may not align with what you've learned here."

"That's why I need to go." The words came out harder than Justin intended. His father's jaw tightened almost imperceptibly, a flicker of something that might have been hurt, before it disappeared.

Roland studied him with that careful expression, as though trying to see something just beneath the surface. Justin felt the old frustration stir in his chest: his father always searching for cracks, always waiting for him to prove himself unready.

"You've changed since the council," Roland said quietly. Only observation. No accusation.

Justin let the words settle. Part of him wanted to reach across the distance between them and explain something he couldn't quite articulate even to himself. He kept his voice even. "I'm trying to understand what's required of me."

"And you believe Malric can teach you that." Roland's tone had gone neutral in a way that felt worse than anger.

"I believe he can show me something I haven't seen." Justin held his father's gaze and willed him to understand, knowing the words were inadequate.

Roland didn't answer immediately. He stood at the desk with one hand resting on the letter, his gaze unfocused, not looking at Justin, not looking at anything, just working through something in that quiet way he had when he was reconciling what he felt with what he knew to be reasonable. The sound of boots crossing the courtyard below drifted up through the glass. Somewhere, a horse shifted and stamped.

Justin waited, his heart beating harder than it should, caught between hope and the old dread of disappointing the man who had taught him everything he knew about what it meant to be good.

Finally Roland spoke, testing each word before releasing it. "I don't have a reason to forbid this. Malric is a loyal vassal, Thornmoor is part of Meridia, you're old enough to travel with an escort, and you're right that a future king should understand how his lords govern." He paused. Something crossed his face, something that looked almost like confusion. "But something about this troubles me, and I can't name what it is."

Justin's chest tightened. "What troubles you?"

Roland shook his head, his hand lifting from the letter to press at his temple. "I don't know, and that's what makes it worse. I have no logical objection, no concrete reason to say no. Just this feeling that sits in my chest like a stone." He looked at Justin again. "I can't explain it."

"Father, if there's a specific concern—"

"There isn't, and that's the problem." Firm, not harsh. "I've spent my life making decisions based on reason and prayer, on what can be seen and understood. But this..." He trailed off, his jaw working around words that wouldn't quite form.

"But what?"

Roland was silent for a long moment, the battle plain behind his eyes: duty warring with instinct, reason struggling against some nameless dread that had no foundation in fact but refused to be dismissed.

Then he exhaled slowly and straightened. When he spoke again, his voice carried the finality of a decision made against his own better judgment. "You will leave tomorrow morning, and Captain Aldric will escort you. But you will stay no more than a fortnight."

Relief moved through Justin like warm water, washing out the tension in his shoulders. "Thank you."

"Strength without virtue consumes itself," Roland said quietly, his gaze holding his son's with an intensity that turned the words from advice to warning. "Remember that. Whatever you see in Thornmoor, whatever Malric shows you, remember what strength is for."

"I won't forget."

Roland nodded once, a gesture that held both blessing and resignation, then turned back to the window as though the conversation had already closed.

"I'll be praying that God is with you," he said, softer now. "And that you come home safely, my boy."

Justin bowed and left, closing the door quietly behind him.

Behind him, Roland stayed at the window, his silhouette dark against the gray light, looking north and wondering why he felt like he'd just made the wrong decision.

They left at dawn. The gates of Highstone swung open onto the northern road, and Justin rode through them with Captain Aldric and four guards. Cold bit through his cloak immediately, a real mountain cold, not the gentled chill of the castle, and the frost on the grass caught the early light with every blade edged in silver. The banners above the gatehouse snapped in the wind with a sound like a thrown card.

Justin looked back once. The castle rose behind him, white stone luminous in the low sun, the chapel tower, the training yard, the high windows of his father's study. The chapel bells would be ringing for morning prayer, and he wondered for a moment whether Elayne would be there. The thought was ridiculous. He pushed it away.

He faced forward and didn't look back again.

The road climbed steadily into the foothills, and for the

first few hours the land was familiar: ordered fields, stone walls, villages with smoke curling from chimneys and children calling to one another in the yards. But the landscape changed as they rode higher. Fields grew sparse, villages shrank, walls went unrepaired. And then, near midday, they reached the tree line.

Justin pulled his horse to a stop.

The forest ahead was burned.

Not recently. Weeks ago, maybe longer. But the damage was still absolute. Blackened trunks rose like skeletal fingers against the gray sky. The ground was scorched bare, no undergrowth, no new growth, nothing but ash and charred wood climbing the slope. And there was a smell to it, not the good smell of woodsmoke or hearth fire, but something colder than that, something dead. The smell of ash that has been rained on and dried and rained on again, a smell with nothing left in it.

"Mountain fire," Captain Aldric said, riding up beside him. "Happens sometimes in dry summers. Lightning strike, most likely."

Justin studied the trees. They weren't just burned. They were twisted, bent and warped as if the heat had been so intense it softened the wood before it burned.

Lightning doesn't do that.

"It wasn't a dry summer," he said.

Aldric glanced at him, expression unchanged. "No. But the mountains are strange. Sulfur vents, hot springs. Could've been anything."

Justin said nothing, and they rode on through the burned forest. Miles of it. The road wound through the char, and the silence was total: no birdsong, no wind moving branches that could still hold wind, just the ring of hooves on stone and the creak of leather tack, and the absence of everything else pressing in on both sides like a held breath.

Near the edge of the burn, something glinted in a ravine below the road. Justin reined his horse and dismounted before Aldric could speak.

"Your Highness—" Aldric started.

Justin was already picking his way down the slope. The ash at the bottom was soft under his boots, finer than wood ash, almost silky, rising in small puffs around his feet. He knelt and brushed the surface back, uncovering the edge of a breastplate, or part of one. The metal was warped, its edges fused into the rock beneath it. Pre-Unification design, the kind his tutors had shown him in history texts.

"Scavengers," Aldric called down from the road. "Old battlefields. The mountains are full of them."

Justin turned the fragment over. Where it had melted smoothest, the steel still caught light, smooth as river clay fired in a kiln, not scorched but *liquefied*. He set it down and climbed back up, and they rode on in silence.

That night they made camp in a clearing near the base of the Graylor range. The mountains rose ahead, dark and jagged against a sky crowded with stars. The air was thinner here and cold, the kind that came in past the fire's warmth and settled into your collar and your wrists. Justin's breath misted every time he exhaled.

The guards built a fire and set a watch. Aldric walked the perimeter. Justin sat near the flames and ate dried meat and bread and tasted neither, his mind drifting: to the great hall at Highstone, warm and bright; to his father's voice in the council chamber; to the burned trees and the melted armor; to the sulfur-and-cold smell that had followed them up from the foothills, faint as a rumor. The fire popped and settled. Pine sap, woodsmoke, the cold pressing in from the dark just beyond the ring of light.

Then, in the deep hours, he heard it.

A sound, low and distant and thunderous, rolling down from the mountains. The grinding of stone on stone, as though the earth itself were shifting beneath the peaks. It went on for several seconds, then stopped. The fire had burned to coals, orange and sullen. One of the guards stirred, looked toward the mountains, and settled back.

Then the sound came again, longer, deeper.

That's not rock. That's not anything natural.

Justin sat up, staring into the darkness. The mountains were only shadows, no movement, no light, nothing but that sound, and then silence.

Aldric appeared beside him. "You heard it."

"Yes."

"Rock fall," Aldric said. "Or a vent opening. The mountains

do that, especially this close to Thornmoor."

Justin looked at him. "That wasn't rock."

Aldric's face was unreadable in the dying firelight. "Then what was it?"

Justin didn't answer.

Aldric waited, then clapped Justin's shoulder once. "Get some sleep, Your Highness. We reach Thornmoor by midday tomorrow."

He walked back to his bedroll. Justin lay down, but sleep didn't come. He stared up at the stars, cold, sharp, indifferent, and listened to the silence that had replaced the sound. He knew, with the kind of knowing that lives in the gut rather than the head, that whatever had made that noise was not rock, not wind, not anything born of the ordinary world. And he knew, just as clearly, that nothing would keep him from riding north in the morning.

Morning came cold and gray. They broke camp without much talk and rode higher, the road narrowing as the trees thinned to nothing. The stone under the horses' hooves changed color and texture, black basalt now, volcanic rock sharp-edged and glassy, spreading up the slopes in frozen rivers where the old fire had run. Justin's horse picked its way carefully, hooves clicking against the hard surface.

He had read about it: the Graylor range was old, older than the kingdoms, older than the Unification. The mountains had been fire once, long ago, and the land still remembered.

By midday, they crested a ridge.

Thornmoor.

The fortress rose from the mountainside like a scar. Dark basalt walls, seamless and sheer, built directly into the rock as though the mountain had expelled it in some ancient convulsion. No banners flew from its towers, no color softened its edges, just black stone, iron fittings, and narrow windows like arrow slits that watched their approach with cold indifference. The air here was thin and carried a faint chemical edge, not quite sulfur but something in that family, something that reminded Justin that the ground under his boots had once been the inside of a volcano.

The gates stood open.

No guards at the entrance. No horns. No one came forward to meet them, only the open gates and a silence that was different from ordinary quiet, deeper and more deliberate, the silence of a place that had been like this for a long time and was not uncomfortable with it. Justin's chest tightened. He had ridden through doubt and his father's half-spoken warnings to reach this place, and here it was, exactly as he had imagined it and somehow more imposing than any description could have prepared him for.

Aldric reined his horse. "We'll wait here for the duke's escort."

Before he finished speaking, a figure appeared in the gateway.

Malric stood alone, hands clasped behind his back. His gray cloak hung motionless despite the mountain wind that tugged at Justin's own clothes, at his banner, at everything else around him. He didn't smile. He didn't bow. He didn't speak; he simply waited, and the sight of him sent a strange current through Justin's chest: the recognition that he had arrived, at last, at the place where everything might change.

Justin dismounted. His boots struck the black basalt with a hard, flat sound. He walked forward until he stopped at the threshold.

Malric inclined his head. His voice was calm, unhurried, the voice of a man who had known all along that Justin would come. "Prince Justin. Welcome to Thornmoor."

Justin looked past him into the courtyard: dark stone, iron fixtures, narrow corridors swallowed by shadow. No warmth. No light. No music. Only order, and certainty, and the mountain cold settling across his shoulders like a hand.

He stepped through the gates.

The threshold was behind him now, and the road back seemed, suddenly, very far away.

- Chapter V -

The courtyard at Thornmoor was nothing like the training yard at Highstone, where laughter and banter between drills filled the air, where sergeants shouted corrections with voices that carried warmth as much as authority.

Here there was just movement.

Justin stood on a narrow balcony overlooking the main courtyard, watching the Thornmoor legion drill in the gray morning light. Malric had left him here without explanation, saying only that he would return shortly. The stone railing under Justin's hands was cold, slick with condensation that smelled faintly of iron.

Below, two hundred men moved in perfect unison.

They wore black leather and mail, their helms identical, their boots striking stone in synchronized rhythm. No one called cadence. No one gave commands. They simply moved. Pivot. Strike. Advance. Withdraw. Like a single organism with two hundred limbs.

The courtyard itself was severe. Black basalt walls rose on all sides, unbroken except for narrow windows and iron-banded doors. No tapestries. No carved stone. No chapel bells or garden walls visible beyond.

At Highstone, the training yard opened onto the inner bailey, where servants crossed with laundry and bread, where children played near the stables, where the chapel tower rose warm and golden in the afternoon sun.

Here there was only stone. And iron. And the measured strike of boots on basalt.

Justin watched a column of soldiers execute a flanking maneuver. They moved without hesitation, each man's position determined by the man beside him, the formation flowing like water around an invisible obstacle.

No one shouted. No one corrected.

The system itself was the correction.

A soldier in the third rank, young, maybe sixteen, missed his step during a turn. His boot came down half a beat late, a stumble that broke the seamless coordination like a pebble dropped into glass. He recovered immediately, his face draining of color, but the damage had been done. Every eye in the courtyard had seen it.

The formation didn't stop. It continued its mechanical precision as though nothing had happened. But an officer at the edge of the courtyard, a man in a gray cloak with a captain's insignia, made a single gesture with his hand. Sharp and final.

Two soldiers stepped out of formation without a word, flanking the young man on either side. They didn't grab him or speak. Their presence was enough. The three of them walked together toward the far wall.

The rest of the legion continued drilling. Their boots struck stone in perfect rhythm, indifferent to the boy being led away.

Justin leaned forward. His hands gripped the cold iron railing hard enough that his knuckles went white.

The young soldier stood at attention against the wall, his back rigid, fighting to hold himself still. The two escorts stepped back, leaving him alone and exposed. The captain approached with a deliberate slowness that made Justin's stomach turn. His face was utterly calm as he removed a thick leather strap from his belt.

Three strikes across the soldier's open palms.

Each one landed with a crack that echoed off the basalt walls, the sound sharp enough to make Justin flinch from the balcony above. The young man didn't cry out, though his jaw clenched so hard Justin could see the muscles jumping beneath the skin. His hands trembled after the second blow, fingers curling involuntarily before he forced them open again for the third strike. This time the strap broke skin. A bright line of red ran down the boy's wrist.

Sixteen. He looked about sixteen.

When it was finished, the captain stepped back and waited, expression unchanged. The soldier, his palms already swelling, brought his hand up in a salute that took visible effort to hold steady. The captain returned it with mechanical courtesy, then turned and walked away as though nothing of consequence had occurred. The boy made his way back to formation on legs that looked barely capable of holding him upright.

The whole thing had taken less than a minute.

Justin's chest tightened. Not from horror. Not from outrage. From recognition.

The punishment hadn't been personal. The captain's face had shown no anger. No satisfaction. The young soldier hadn't been humiliated or cast out. He'd made an error. The error had been corrected. The system had continued.

At Highstone, a missed step would have earned a sharp word from the sergeant, maybe an extra lap around the yard. The other soldiers would have laughed or offered encouragement while the mistake dissolved into the noise and warmth of the day.

Here, there was no noise to absorb it. Only consequence.

"Efficient, isn't it?"

Justin turned to find Malric standing in the doorway behind him, hands clasped loosely before him, gray eyes steady and untroubled.

Justin straightened instinctively. "Your men are disciplined."

"They are predictable," Malric said, stepping onto the balcony. His boots made no sound against the stone. "Discipline is merely the visible result of that predictability. The structure beneath it is what matters." He gestured toward the courtyard below, where the legion had already shifted into a new formation, shield wall assembled, spears leveled, each man's position exact to the inch. "At Highstone, your father's men love him. They would die for him without question. I don't doubt that for a moment. But love is a variable, Your Highness. It waxes and wanes with the seasons. Depends on mood, on circumstance, on whether a man slept well the night before or received a letter from home."

He paused, letting the words settle.

"Men obey what they fear losing," Malric said.

Justin looked at him. "And what do your men fear losing?"

"Their place." Malric said it simply, as though it required no elaboration. "Their role within the structure. A man who knows his position, who understands the consequences of failure and the rewards of precision, doesn't require affection. He requires certainty."

Below, the formation executed a complex maneuver, rotating shields and advancing in staggered lines, each movement dependent on the timing of the man before. A choreography of steel and discipline.

"Affection fades," Malric said, his voice carrying neither coldness nor cruelty, just the steady assurance of a man explaining mathematics. "But fear remains."

Justin turned back to the courtyard. "And if a man resents it?"

"Then he leaves, or he fails, and the structure removes him." Malric tilted his head slightly. "But most men don't. Most are grateful, because they know where they stand and what's expected of them. There's no confusion, no favoritism, no wondering whether their commander woke in a foul mood."

He gestured toward the young soldier, now back in formation. The boy's movements were precise and deliberate.

"That boy made a mistake and was corrected. Now he's returned to his place. Tomorrow, he won't make the same mistake, and the men around him who saw the consequence won't make it either. No one had to shout or explain. The system taught them."

Justin's hands tightened on the railing.

He wanted to argue. Wanted to say that men weren't mechanisms, that loyalty built on fear was brittle, that his father's way, leading with virtue, with trust, with the example of righteousness, was stronger.

But he had seen the Highstone guard laugh during drills. Had seen them arrive late to muster, offering excuses. Had seen his father's patience tested again and again by men who loved him but didn't always obey him.

And he had seen, just now, two hundred men move as one.

It worked. That was the trouble with it. It worked.

"You're thinking," Malric observed, and there was something almost pleased in his tone.

Justin glanced at him, trying to keep his voice steady. "Is that permitted?"

A faint smile touched Malric's mouth. It didn't reach his eyes. "It's required."

He stepped back toward the doorway with the unhurried confidence of a man who knew exactly how much ground he'd gained. "I'll leave you to your observations, Prince

Justin. Supper is at sundown. A servant will show you to the hall."

He paused at the threshold. The pause itself felt deliberate.

"Your father governs by inspiration," he said quietly, and the words carried an edge Justin couldn't quite name. "I govern by structure. Both can build kingdoms. But only one can hold them when the inspiration fades."

He left. The silence behind him was heavier than it should have been.

Justin stood alone on the balcony, watching the legion drill in perfect, unthinking unison. Two hundred men who never hesitated. Never questioned. Never missed a step, because the cost of missing was written in the blood on a boy's palms drying in the cold morning air.

He wondered why the sight made him feel so hollow.

That night, Justin sat in the chamber Malric had given him. A narrow room. Single window. A bed, a desk, a lamp. The walls were bare basalt, no tapestries or icons, just stone and iron and the faint smell of lamp oil.

He'd tried to pray before bed, the way he always did at Highstone. But the words felt distant here, as though the stone walls swallowed them before they could rise.

So he thought instead.

He thought about the young soldier and the three strikes across his palms. The captain's expressionless face. The way the system had corrected itself without anger, without chaos. He thought about Malric's words. *Men obey what they fear losing.* Was it true?

At Highstone, the guards obeyed his father because they loved him, because they believed in his vision of justice and mercy. But what happened when love wasn't enough?

Malric's system didn't depend on belief. It depended on structure, on consequence, on the certainty that every action had a predictable result and every man knew what that result would be. It was brilliant in its cold efficiency.

Justin leaned back against the wall and stared at the ceiling.

He understood now why Malric's influence had grown, why lords across Meridia listened when he spoke, why even his father had sent him here to learn. Malric's way worked. It wasn't righteous. Wasn't warm. But it was effective, and effectiveness had a gravity of its own.

He closed his eyes.

Then the sound came.

Low at first. A rumble from deep in the mountains, like thunder rolling through stone. Then it grew louder, swelling into a roar that rattled the window in its frame and sent the lamp flame flickering wildly. Justin felt it in his chest, in his bones, in the floor beneath his feet. Something cold began to coil in his stomach — something he had never felt at Highstone. This wasn't wind. Wasn't a rockslide. *It was alive.* The realization crept up his spine like a hand laid against bare skin.

He stood, heart hammering, and crossed to the window on

legs that felt uncertain beneath him. The mountains were dark. No movement. No light. Just the sound fading now, echoing through the peaks, leaving behind a silence that felt heavier than what had come before.

Then a voice from behind him, quiet and unhurried, and Justin realized with a cold certainty that the man had been standing there for some time. Watching him listen to the mountains.

"They remind us who holds them," Malric said from the doorway, his gray cloak lost in shadow. He hadn't knocked. Hadn't announced himself. He had simply chosen the moment to make his presence known.

Justin turned. "What was that?"

Malric's expression remained perfectly still, as though the question had been expected. "A reminder," he said, and stepped into the room, hands clasped behind his back. "You'll hear it again. Perhaps tomorrow, perhaps not for days. But you will hear it, and each time you'll wonder whether it comes of its own accord or because it has been called."

He moved to the window and looked out at the dark peaks with the ease of a man surveying something he understood completely. Something that understood him in return.

"Some things can't be governed by affection, Prince Justin. Men, beasts, the things that dwell in deep places. They respond to strength, to certainty, to the knowledge that there exists a power greater than themselves." He turned, his gray eyes steady in the lamplight. "Your father believes men can be inspired to goodness. I believe they must be compelled toward it. And I have the means to do so."

He paused. In that pause, Justin sensed the unspoken truth: that Malric possessed something, some force, some ancient authority, that he would not hesitate to use.

"The question you must answer for yourself," Malric continued, his voice quiet but unyielding, "is which approach will hold when the mountains wake and something must be there to quiet them again. Will it be your father's prayers? Or will it be the hand that knows how to reach into the darkness and make it obey?"

He walked to the door. Paused at the threshold just long enough to let the implication take root.

"Sleep well, Prince Justin."

Then he was gone.

Justin stood alone in the narrow room. The lamp flame had steadied, but the echo of the roar still trembled in the stone beneath his feet, and the cold had crept closer, and the prayers he'd tried to speak an hour ago felt like they belonged to someone else's kingdom.

- Chapter VI -

Justin woke before dawn, though he hadn't meant to.

Sleep had come in fragments. Brief stretches of darkness broken by the memory of that sound, that roar from the mountains, and each time he woke he listened for it again. The castle remained silent.

By the time gray light touched his window, he gave up trying. He dressed and left his chamber to wander the empty corridors of Thornmoor. No servants moved through the halls at this hour. No guards stood at the interior doors. The castle felt less like a fortress and more like a mechanism that had paused between cycles, waiting.

Justin walked without direction, his boots quiet on the stone. The severe lines of everything pressed in around him. No curves. No ornament. Just black basalt walls broken only by narrow windows and iron sconces. The doors were thick oak banded with iron, their hinges heavy and functional. At Highstone, even the servants' quarters had carved lintels or painted shutters. Here there was only stone and iron and purpose.

He turned down a corridor he hadn't explored before, one that sloped slightly downward, the ceiling lower than the main halls. The air smelled different here. Older, somehow. Less used. The cold had a mineral edge to it, like standing inside a cave.

At the end of the corridor, he found a door smaller than the others, set into an alcove. The wood was dark with age, the iron handle worn smooth by hands that no longer came. Above the lintel, a simple cross was carved into the stone.

Justin stopped.

A chapel. In this place.

He pushed the door open. The hinges creaked, loud in the stillness.

Inside, the chapel was narrow and cold. Two rows of wooden pews faced a small stone altar. The walls were bare except for a single tapestry behind the altar, faded blue, depicting a shepherd and a lamb. Three stained glass windows lined the eastern wall, their colors muted in the early light.

Dust covered the pews. The candles on the altar sat unlit, their wax old and cracked. The air smelled of cold stone and the particular stillness of rooms where no one breathes.

At Highstone, the chapel was the heart of the castle, where bells rang three times daily and servants stopped to pray between tasks. His father knelt there every morning before dawn, head bowed, hands steady.

Here, the chapel felt like a room someone had forgotten to close.

Justin stepped inside. His boots left prints in the dust.

He walked slowly between the pews, his hand trailing along the wood. No one had sat here in weeks. Maybe months. The tapestry behind the altar was fraying at the edges, and one of the stained glass windows had a crack running through its center.

He stopped at the front and looked up at the windows. He recognized the scenes: the calling of the disciples, the feeding of the multitude, the empty tomb. Simple images, rendered in glass that had once been bright but now seemed dull.

"I wondered if you would find this place."

Justin spun, his heart lurching, one hand reaching for the pew beside him to steady himself.

Malric stood in the doorway, gray cloak dark against the stone. Justin couldn't say how long he'd been there or how he'd arrived without a sound. He didn't enter, didn't move forward. He simply stood at the threshold with his hands clasped, as though he'd been watching for some time and saw no reason to explain himself.

"I didn't mean to intrude," Justin said, and hated how his voice came out unsteady.

"You haven't." Malric stepped inside at last. His boots were somehow silent despite the dust that had announced Justin's every step. He glanced around the chapel with the same detached interest he might give a storage room. "It's open to all who wish to use it."

"But no one does," Justin said.

Malric's mouth curved slightly. "No," he agreed. He walked to the nearest pew and ran his finger along the back, leaving a clean line in the dust. "Your father keeps a chapel at Highstone, does he not?"

"He does."

"And he prays there. Daily, I imagine." Malric studied the dust on his finger, then brushed it away. "Faith is for men who can afford gentleness."

The words weren't harsh or mocking. Just stated, like an observation about the weather.

Something hot flared behind Justin's ribs. "You think my father is gentle?"

"I think your father governs a kingdom that allows him to be," Malric said, turning to face him. Those steady gray eyes again. "Highstone is prosperous. Its borders are secure. Its people are fed. In such a place, a man can kneel and pray and trust the kingdom won't collapse while his eyes are closed."

He gestured toward the chapel. The dusty pews. The unlit candles. The forgotten altar. The dismissiveness of the motion made Justin's jaw clench.

"Here, we don't have that luxury."

Justin wanted to argue. Wanted to say that faith wasn't a luxury at all. That his father's strength came from his certainty in something greater than himself. That prayer wasn't weakness but the foundation of all true governance. That a man who had buried his wife not three months past and still rose each morning to kneel before God was stronger than any lord who trusted only in his own hands.

But the words caught in his throat. Tangled with grief and doubt and the terrible suspicion that Malric wasn't entirely wrong.

What would happen to Highstone if the kingdom weren't strong enough to hold itself while his father knelt?

Malric watched him. Something flickered in his expression, too quick to name but unmistakable in its satisfaction. He'd seen the doubt take root.

"I don't forbid prayer, Prince Justin. I don't mock it. But I don't depend on it either." His voice was quiet and even. "A man who waits for divine intervention while his borders burn is a fool. A man who acts, and prays afterward if he wishes, is a king."

He walked toward the door, unhurried, pausing only at the threshold to glance back.

"You're welcome to use this place," he said. The words were almost gentle. Almost kind. Somehow that made them cut deeper. "But don't mistake comfort for clarity."

Then he was gone, and Justin stood alone with the silence and the weight of everything he'd just conceded without meaning to.

He looked at the altar with its unlit candles and faded tapestry, and thought of his father kneeling in the chapel at Highstone, head bowed, lips moving in silent prayer. He'd witnessed that sight a hundred times. A thousand. Before every council. Every departure. Before the battle at Greymarch, when the northern lords had risen in rebellion and Roland had ridden out with three hundred men.

Justin's mind drifted back a few short years, to the night before that battle. He'd watched his father kneel with his armor already on and his sword laid across his knees. Roland hadn't prayed for victory. He'd prayed for wisdom. For the resolve to do what was right even if it cost him everything. It was only months after the queen's death, and Justin had wondered then if his father was praying for the will to keep going at all — to lead a kingdom while his heart was still breaking. But Roland had ridden out at dawn regardless. The rebellion had ended without a single life lost, because he'd offered the lords terms they could accept without shame.

Justin had asked him afterward how he'd known what to do. Roland had smiled in that quiet way he'd learned since becoming a widower, since grief had taught him a different kind of patience. "I didn't," he'd said. "But I trusted that the answer would come."

And it had. Just as answers had come in the year after his mother's death, when the kingdom might have fractured under Roland's sorrow but instead held steady, guided by a king who knelt each morning and rose with purpose.

Justin knelt.

The movement felt awkward and uncertain, nothing like his father's practiced grace. His knees hit the cold stone, and the chill went straight through his trousers. He folded his hands, unsure of what to pray for. Clarity, maybe. Or forgiveness for doubting.

He closed his eyes and let the thought form slowly. *I don't know what I'm supposed to see here. I don't know if Malric is right or if my father is right or if they're both right in different ways. I don't know if I'm strong enough to choose.*

The chapel was silent. No answer came.

Justin kept his eyes closed, his hands folded, his breath slow and steady.

Then the light changed.

He felt it before he saw it. A shift in the air. A warmth that hadn't been there before, creeping across his skin like breath against the back of his neck. The smell of the room changed too, the cold mineral stone giving way to something sharper. Hotter. Like iron left too long in a forge.

When he opened his eyes, the stained glass windows were glowing.

Not with the weak gray dawn struggling through the eastern sky. With something else entirely. A radiance that pulsed and shimmered as though something living moved behind the colored panes.

A shadow passed across the center window. Massive. Winged. Its shape was distorted by the ancient glass but unmistakable in its terrible grace. The curve of wings that spanned the width of the frame. The serpentine length of a body that went on and on. The whip-like suggestion of a tail trailing behind like smoke.

Heat rolled through the chapel in waves. The air shimmered and bent. The blues and golds of the stained glass rippled as though the stone itself were melting. Justin could not move. Could not breathe. He could only watch as the shadow crossed from one window to the next with a fluid, predatory slowness that made his blood go cold even as the air burned.

Then, as suddenly as it had come, the shadow was gone.

With it went the light and the heat. What remained was the cold gray chapel and the sound of Justin's ragged breathing echoing off the stone walls.

He stood frozen, staring at the windows. Nothing moved. No shadow. No light. No shimmer of heat distorting the air. Just cracked glass and faded colors catching the weak dawn. Ordinary and still.

He crossed to the windows slowly, half-expecting the heat to return, and pressed his hand against the center pane where the shadow had passed. The glass was cold beneath his palm. Undisturbed. He checked the sill and found only dust, thick and settled, untouched by wind or movement.

That was real. He was certain. That was real.

Or had his mind, exhausted from sleeplessness and prayer, conjured the vision from nothing? From fear, perhaps. From the weight of everything Malric had said.

He turned and strode to the chapel door, pulling it open with more force than necessary. The corridor beyond stretched empty and silent. No sound of wings. No sign that anything had passed through these halls at all.

Justin stood in the doorway, breath uneven, hands trembling despite his efforts to steady them.

Hadn't it?

He stepped back into the chapel and closed the door, leaning against it. The windows were dark now, colors muted in the growing dawn. The tapestry hung motionless. The candles remained unlit, their wicks black and cold.

He couldn't explain what he had seen. But he knew he couldn't tell Malric. And he couldn't tell his father. Because if it had been real, he didn't know what it meant. What it said about Thornmoor. About the power Malric claimed to wield. About the path Justin was being asked to walk.

And if it hadn't been real, if his mind was conjuring visions of winged shadows and impossible heat, then what did that say about him?

He left the chapel and walked back through the corridors. The memory of it turned over and over in his mind, but it was already slipping, becoming less tangible with each step he took away from that cold gray room. Like smoke. Like something that didn't want to be held.

By the time he reached his chamber, the sun had risen fully. The mountains beyond Thornmoor's walls were quiet and still.

- Chapter VII -

The bells of Highstone rang as Justin rode through the outer gate. Three clear notes carrying across the courtyard the way they always did when someone returned. Warm. Familiar. Something in his chest loosened at the sound.

Home.

The word felt strange now. Not wrong, exactly. Just different, as though the two weeks at Thornmoor had shifted the meaning of it without his noticing until this moment, when the bells rang and he realized how much had changed in the space between their ringing. Nothing else unusual had happened after that morning in the chapel. No more shadows. No more visions. Only Malric's voice day after day, patient and certain, reshaping the way Justin saw everything until the questions he'd arrived with no longer seemed like questions at all but answers he'd simply been too young to recognize before.

He dismounted in the courtyard and handed his reins to a groom. The cobblestones were warm under his boots after the cold basalt of Thornmoor, and the air smelled of bread and forge smoke and something green from the gardens beyond the wall. The groom smiled, his face weathered and kind. "Good to have you back, my lord."

Justin nodded. He did not smile.

The courtyard bustled with the usual morning work. Servants carrying water. Guards changing shifts. A blacksmith's hammer ringing from the forge, the smell of hot iron drifting across the cobblestones. Everything moved with the easy rhythm of a place that knew itself. No formations. No drills. Just people doing their work without fear of correction.

It looked softer than he remembered. Almost careless in its ease.

"Justin."

He turned to find his father standing at the top of the steps, cloak dark against the pale stone. Roland descended quickly, his stride long and steady, and when he reached Justin he pulled him into an embrace that was warm and somehow too much all at once.

"Welcome home."

Justin returned the embrace, but his arms felt stiff and formal, as though they'd forgotten the gesture. Roland pulled back and studied him. For a moment neither spoke. His father's eyes moved over Justin's face, not searching exactly, but noticing. Taking in something that had shifted in the space of two weeks. His expression remained calm, but something changed in it. A question he didn't ask but that hung between them.

"How was the journey?" Roland said finally.

"Uneventful."

"And Thornmoor?"

Justin hesitated. He felt the weight of everything he might

say and chose the simplest answer. "Impressive."

Roland nodded slowly. He didn't press, didn't ask the questions Justin could see forming behind his steady gaze. Just stood there, hand still on Justin's shoulder. Patient. Warm. Waiting.

The weight of it made Justin uncomfortable in a way he couldn't name.

He shifted, glancing toward the keep. "I should see to my things."

Roland's hand dropped. He nodded once. "Of course. We'll speak later."

Justin walked toward the keep, leaving his father standing at the base of the steps. Behind him, the bells rang again. Softer now. Fading into the morning air.

He saw her crossing the courtyard with two of her ladies.

Her gown was a deep blue that caught the morning light, and something in his chest tightened in a way that had nothing to do with Thornmoor or duty or the clarity he thought he'd found there. She was speaking to one of the women, something that made the other laugh. But when she turned and saw him, the ease in her expression shifted to something more formal. More careful.

"Your Highness." She inclined her head, her companions doing the same. "Welcome back."

"Lady Elayne." Justin nodded, equally formal. He had no reason to stop. Should have continued past her toward the keep. But his feet wouldn't move, and his mind went blank of anything sensible to say. "You were at the balcony," he said, the words out before he could catch them. "Before I left. During the sparring."

The words landed between them, and in the silence that followed, something clicked into place. The fountain. The evening before he'd ridden out for Thornmoor. He had seen her since then. Had stood three paces from her and fumbled through a conversation so awkward he'd replayed it twice on the ride north. And here he was, bringing up the sparring as though the balcony were the last time they'd crossed paths.

Brilliant, Justin. Truly.

Elayne's expression shifted. A faint color rose along her cheekbones, and she glanced at her companions before looking back at him. "Yes," she said, her voice a careful half-step above a murmur. "The sparring. It was... quite something."

She said it the way someone agrees with a wrong answer to spare the person who gave it. Polite. Deliberate. Her gaze stayed steady, but something around her mouth tightened with the effort of not acknowledging what they both knew.

She dismissed her ladies with a subtle gesture. When they'd moved away, she turned back to him with an expression he couldn't quite read. "I was."

"You watched." Another obvious statement.

His eyes dropped to the cobblestones between them. He couldn't hold her gaze. He'd stood before Malric's cold scrutiny without flinching, had endured the man's silence and judgment in that chapel without looking away. Yet here, before this young woman, he felt himself retreating like a chastened boy. The realization sent a hot flush of irritation through him.

"You fought well that day," she said, and he forced himself to look up, jaw tight.

Something in her tone unsettled him. Not quite approval. Not quite question. As though she were asking something he didn't know how to answer, and the clarity he'd carried back from Thornmoor felt suddenly fragile.

"And now you've returned from Thornmoor," she said.

"I have."

She studied him a moment. Her gaze was not prying but observant, and he couldn't look away from it.

"I hope it was instructive," she said finally.

"It was."

A pause stretched between them. The courtyard sounds receded. The clatter of hooves, the call of guards changing watch, all of it fading until there was only the weight of her attention and his growing awareness beneath it.

"My father speaks highly of Lord Malric," she said. Her voice carried a careful neutrality that felt more pointed than direct criticism. "He says Thornmoor is the most efficiently run holding in the realm."

"It is."

"That must be… impressive to see."

Something cold moved through Justin's chest. She was leading him somewhere he didn't want to go, and the way she said it, not quite admiration, not quite criticism, made his shoulders tense.

"It was necessary," he said. He heard the defensiveness in his own voice. "Order must be maintained."

"Yes." Her expression didn't change, but something flickered in her eyes. "Necessary."

The word hung between them.

Heat rose in his neck. "You disapprove."

"I didn't say that."

"You didn't have to." Sharper than he'd intended. Edged with an anger that surprised him, as though she'd touched something raw he hadn't known was there.

She tilted her head slightly. There was something maddeningly composed about the gesture, and his frustration spiked because she seemed entirely unmoved by his irritation. "I only wonder what you learned there, Your Highness. That's all."

"I learned how a lord maintains order. How he protects his people."

"I see." She was quiet a moment. "And did Duke Malric teach you that himself?"

Justin's hands curled into fists at his sides, nails biting into his palms. She was doing it again. Asking questions that sounded innocent but felt like traps, and he couldn't tell whether the trap was real or whether he was simply too raw to hear anything without suspicion. "He didn't need to teach it. I saw it."

"Of course." She picked up her skirts, preparing to move past him. "Forgive me. I shouldn't have presumed to question you."

But something in her voice made it clear she wasn't apologizing at all. She'd said exactly what she'd meant to say, and his reaction had told her everything she'd wanted to know.

She walked away, her ladies rejoining her at the entrance to the keep.

Justin watched her go. The blue of her gown disappeared through the archway, and the courtyard felt emptier for it. Frustration churned in his chest. At his own clumsy defensiveness. At the way she'd made him feel like a boy pretending at authority. But also an awareness of her he didn't want and couldn't dismiss. A nagging sense that she'd seen through him in a way Malric never had, because Malric had only looked for strength while she'd been looking for something else entirely.

Her quiet questions had shaken him more than Malric's harsh judgments. Her careful words had made the clarity he'd found at Thornmoor feel suddenly uncertain.

He didn't like not understanding things. Didn't like the way his thoughts kept circling back to her expression, her tone, the implications he couldn't grasp but felt pressing against him.

The stables smelled of hay and leather and horses. The familiar scents wrapped around him as he walked between the stalls, his boots quiet on the packed dirt. Horses shifted and snorted, their breath warm in the cool air. A few nuzzled his hand as he passed.

At the far end, a boy was struggling with a saddle. Thin frame bent over the task, movements clumsy as he tried to settle it onto a mare's back. The girth strap had twisted, and he fumbled with it while the mare shifted impatiently beneath his hands.

The boy tugged harder. The saddle slipped.

"Stop."

Justin's voice cut through the stable, and the boy froze. Justin walked toward him with measured steps, not hurrying, moving with the same controlled precision he'd seen in Malric's officers.

"What are you doing?"

The boy's face flushed. "I was saddling her, my lord. For the afternoon patrol."

"You were fumbling."

"I'm sorry, my lord. The strap—"

"The strap twisted because you didn't check it before you lifted the saddle." Justin's voice was calm. Clinical. Each word deliberate. "That's how errors cost lives. A twisted girth fails under weight. The rider falls. The horse bolts. Do you understand?"

The boy nodded quickly, eyes wide.

"Do it again," Justin said. "Properly."

The boy's hands shook as he lifted the saddle off the mare's back and laid it on the ground, checking the straps with jerky, nervous movements. Justin watched in silence as he lifted the saddle again, more carefully this time, and settled it onto the mare's back before fastening the girth strap with fumbling but functional fingers.

"Better," Justin said, and turned to leave.

"Where did you learn to speak that way?"

He stopped.

His father stood in the stable doorway, arms crossed, expression unreadable. Sunlight fell across his shoulders, and behind him the courtyard was bright and warm, and the contrast between that warmth and the cold thing Justin had just done settled over him before he could push it away.

Justin's chest tightened. "I was correcting him."

"I saw." Roland stepped inside, boots quiet on the dirt, and glanced at the boy still standing beside the mare, face pale. "You may go, Conn."

The boy nodded quickly and hurried out.

Roland waited until he was gone. Then he looked at Justin.

"Where did you learn to speak that way?" he asked again.

Justin's jaw tightened. "I was being clear. He needed correction."

"He needed instruction," Roland said quietly. "Not fear."

"Fear keeps him careful."

The words came out before Justin could stop them. They hung in the air between them, and for the first time since Thornmoor, Justin heard them the way someone else might — not as wisdom, but as something borrowed. Something that didn't fit his mouth.

Roland's expression didn't change. He stood there with his arms still crossed.

"Does it?" he said.

Justin said nothing.

Roland walked closer and stopped a few feet away, his gaze never leaving Justin's face.

"That boy has worked in these stables for two years," Roland said. "He's careful because he cares about the horses. Because he wants to do well. Not because he's afraid of being corrected."

"He was careless."

"He was learning."

Justin's hands curled into fists. "At Thornmoor, carelessness is corrected immediately. It's efficient. It works."

"Does it?"

The question hung in the air. Roland didn't argue. Didn't lecture. He simply asked.

Justin had no answer.

Roland studied him a moment longer. Then he sighed, his shoulders dropping slightly.

"You sound like Malric," he said quietly.

Justin's breath caught.

Roland's expression softened. Not with disappointment. Not with anger. With something that looked like sadness.

"I'm not saying you're wrong to want clarity," Roland said, "or to expect competence. But there's a difference between correction and cruelty. Between discipline and fear."

"I wasn't cruel."

"No," Roland agreed. "But you were cold."

He stepped closer and placed a hand on Justin's shoulder.

"Malric governs through fear because he believes men are only as loyal as their terror. I govern through trust because I believe men are capable of more than survival."

He paused.

"Which do you believe?"

Justin wanted to answer. Wanted to say he believed what his father believed. That men were capable of virtue and loyalty and strength without fear.

But the words wouldn't come.

Because he'd seen the legion at Thornmoor. Two hundred men moving as one, without hesitation or question. He'd seen efficiency. Order. Power.

And he'd felt something in himself respond to it.

Roland's hand dropped.

"Think about it," he said quietly.

Then he walked out of the stable, and Justin stood alone with the horses and the smell of hay and the echo of his own voice.

That night, Justin stood at his window and looked out over the courtyard. The chapel bells rang for evening prayer. Servants moved through the halls with voices soft and unhurried. Somewhere in the distance a dog barked. Everything was warm and familiar and safe.

Justin felt like a stranger in it all. The window glass was cool against his forehead when he leaned against it, and the evening air carried the faint smell of wood smoke from the kitchens below.

He thought of Conn's face. The flinch when Justin spoke. The way the boy's hands had shaken as he lifted the saddle again. He thought of Malric's voice in the chapel at Thornmoor. *Faith is for men who can afford gentleness.* And of his father's question. *Which do you believe?*

Justin didn't know.

He had corrected the boy efficiently and clearly, the way Malric's officers corrected their men, and it had worked. Conn had done the task properly the second time. But Justin had heard the tremor in the boy's voice. And he had felt something cold and controlled inside himself that had enjoyed it. Not cruelly. Not with malice. Just the quiet satisfaction of being obeyed.

Justin closed his eyes.

He didn't know which troubled him more. That he had sounded like Malric, or that it had felt so easy.

- Chapter VIII -

____

The messenger arrived at dawn. Justin heard him first: boots hammering stone, voices kept deliberately low in the way that meant something had already gone wrong. He dressed fast, the morning air biting through his shirt before he could pull on his coat, and reached the council chamber just as his father broke the dispatch seal. Roland read without speaking. The set of his shoulders told Justin everything his face didn't yet.

"Whitethorne," Roland said, setting the parchment on the table. "The entire village burned in the night."

The word dropped cold in Justin's chest. "Survivors?"

"Some." His father's voice was measured, careful. "A family of four who fled to the woods when the fires started. An old shepherd. A boy who'd been out hunting late."

Sir Aldric stood near the window with his arms crossed, morning light flat against his back. "How many dead?"

"Thirty-seven. Maybe more." Roland looked down at the parchment again. "The fires were thorough."

Justin moved closer to the table. The room smelled of tallow and old parchment, and somewhere a shutter had been left open. He could feel the morning chill coming in off the stone, working its way through his wool. "What did the survivors see?"

Roland looked up. There was something in his father's gaze Justin couldn't name. Not warning, not caution. Weight. Just that.

Roland's jaw worked before the words came. When they did, they came slowly, as though each one cost something.

"They saw fire and smoke." He paused, his hand still pressed flat against the parchment. "And a shadow with wings that passed over the rooftops before the flames began."

His voice had dropped. Heavier now.

The room went still.

Justin's pulse kicked. "A shadow."

"Briefly, in the dark," Roland said. "They couldn't say more than that."

Sir Aldric exhaled, long and heavy, the sound carrying more resignation than words would have. "Then it's confirmed."

"Nothing is confirmed." Roland said it quietly, though his tone carried the weight of a man who knew how thin that argument had grown. "We have testimony given in fear and darkness. We have destruction. We don't have certainty."

Justin's hands tightened at his sides. *How much more do we need?* "How much more do we need?"

Roland's gaze found him — that steady look Justin had watched settle disputes and quiet rooms for as long as he could remember. Not sharp. Not reproachful. The unhurried certainty of a man who had learned to measure his words before releasing them.

"Enough to act justly," Roland said.

Justin felt it like a rebuke, though there was nothing harsh in his father's tone. Somehow that made it worse.

He repeated the word slowly, let it sit on his tongue, cold and strange. "Justly. Thirty-seven people are dead, and you speak of acting justly toward *that*?"

"We investigate," Roland said. "We send scouts, reinforce the northern villages, but we do not—"

"We wait." Justin cut through his father's sentence, and heard himself do it.

The silence that followed wasn't empty. It was sharp, pressing, filling the space between them with something unspoken. Sir Aldric's head turned. His eyes widened slightly, his posture straightening, as though he'd just witnessed something he needed a moment to believe.

Roland's expression didn't shift. His shoulders drew back, just slightly, just enough.

"Justin," he said. The single word carrying more than a sentence would have.

"We wait while more villages burn." Justin heard the edge in his own voice and didn't stop. "While more families disappear, while whatever is in those mountains learns we'll do nothing." He knew he should stop. He didn't.

Roland's gaze stayed steady, but something had changed in his eyes. Not anger. Recognition.

"We don't wait," Roland said. "We prepare. There's a difference."

"Is there?" Justin stepped forward, heat climbing his neck. "Father, if the people knew we'd respond, if they knew any threat to Meridia would be met with force, this wouldn't have happened."

Sir Aldric's jaw tightened. He glanced at Roland, then back at Justin, his silence pointed now, deliberate.

"You believe that," Roland said. Not a question.

Justin lifted his chin. "I do."

Roland folded his hands on the table. Beneath his calm there was something harder now, something like stone behind a gate. "What force would you use, Justin? Against what enemy? In what place?"

"The mountains," Justin said. "Thornmoor's patrols could sweep the northern range, and Duke Malric has the men and the discipline. If we coordinated—"

"Malric's men aren't ours to command."

"Then we ask. We ally." His voice was rising and he could hear it, feel it rising like heat he couldn't push back down. "We show strength, make it clear that Meridia won't tolerate—"

"Fear," Roland said.

Justin stopped.

"You're describing fear, Justin." His father's voice stayed quiet, unhurried. "You're saying that if we make the people afraid of our response, they won't act against us, and if we make our enemies afraid of our strength, they won't strike."

Roland's gaze was steady. Not angry, not cold. Clear. And beneath the clarity, something else. Justin recognized it even though he didn't want to, even though part of him tried to call it something different. He knew the look. He had seen it directed at others.

Disappointment.

"Yes," Justin said. The word came out firm and controlled. "That's what I'm saying."

Roland nodded slowly, his expression unreadable in the candlelight. "And you learned this at Thornmoor."

"I learned it from watching what works."

"Did you." Not a question. Justin answered anyway.

"Malric's men don't hesitate," he said, his voice gaining strength now. "They act with certainty because they know their lord won't waver. His people are safe because his enemies know the cost of defiance."

"His people are silent," Roland said. The words fell between them like stones. "There's a difference."

Justin's hands curled into fists at his sides. "They're alive."

"For now." The words hung in the air, heavy with everything left unsaid.

Sir Aldric shifted near the window, a silent witness. He didn't speak, but his eyes moved between father and son, watchful.

Roland stood. He didn't raise his voice or move quickly. But the room grew smaller around him, the weight of his presence filling the space. "Justin," he said, measured and deliberate, "do you know what fear does to a ruler?"

Justin said nothing. The candles guttered faintly in a draft, flame bending and steadying.

"It doesn't begin with the people," Roland said. "It begins with the man who wields it. He tells himself it's necessary. Efficient. That it keeps order." He paused. "And then one day he realizes he can't stop. Because the moment he shows mercy, the moment he hesitates, the whole structure collapses."

"That's not—"

"Fear corrupts the ruler first." Roland's voice was quiet but solid, the kind that didn't give ground. "It makes him small. Suspicious. It makes him see every question as rebellion, every delay as weakness. And in the end, it doesn't matter how strong his army is. He's already lost the only battle that matters."

Justin's throat tightened. He forced the words through. "And what battle is that?"

"The one for his own soul."

It hit like a blade. Unexpected, sharp. The words sat in the air of the room, pressed into the silence with the same weight as the cold stone beneath his feet.

Justin wanted to argue — wanted to say his father was wrong, that strength and certainty weren't the same as cruelty, that Malric's order wasn't tyranny. But nothing came. Because somewhere deep in his chest he felt the truth of what Roland had said, and he hated it.

"You think I'm wrong," Roland said. Not a question.

Justin met his father's eyes and held them. "I think you're too careful."

Roland nodded slowly, as though he'd expected exactly this. "Perhaps I am." He glanced at the dispatch on the table, then back. "But I won't rule men by making them small. I won't build a kingdom on the bones of their courage."

"Then what will you build it on?" His voice was colder now, sharper, and he heard it himself. "Hope? Faith? How many people have to die before those aren't enough?"

Sir Aldric drew a sharp, audible breath.

Roland's face didn't change, but something moved through his eyes. Not anger, not disappointment. Recognition.

"I don't know," he said quietly, "but I know what happens when we abandon them."

He looked at Justin for a long moment. Not as a king looks

at a subject, not even as a father looks at a son. As a man looks at something he has lost, and knows he cannot call back.

He turned toward the window. Morning light fell across his shoulders, pale and unhurried, casting his shadow long and thin across the stone floor.

When he spoke again, his voice was calm. Final. "You won't return to Thornmoor."

Justin's breath stopped. "What?"

"You won't visit Duke Malric again. You won't ride his patrols, you won't train with his men." Roland's tone was steady, measured. "That's my command."

Justin went rigid. "Father—"

"I am not angry with you, Justin." Roland turned back, his expression steady and sad in equal measure. "But I will not watch you become something you are not."

"You don't know what I am."

"No," Roland said quietly, "but I know what you could be, and I know what Malric would make of you." He paused, his eyes holding Justin's. "And I know that the boy who stood in this chamber a month ago would not have spoken to his king the way you spoke today."

The words landed in Justin's chest. He had interrupted his father, argued with him, spoken with coldness. Not as a son to a father, but as an equal, or worse, as a superior to someone he no longer respected.

I broke something in this room. The realization came slowly, and it was heavy. Not just the argument, not just the sharp words. He had interrupted his father before the council's witnesses, had spoken with the cold certainty of a man who didn't need to earn the right to be heard. Everyone knew it.

Sir Aldric stood near the window, his face carefully neutral, his eyes troubled.

"Is that all?" Justin's voice came out flat.

Roland studied him for a long moment. Then nodded. "That is all."

Justin turned and walked to the door. His boots echoed on stone, each step sharp and deliberate in the quiet. His hands were steady at his sides. He didn't look back.

Behind him, Sir Aldric's voice was low and careful.

"He is young, my lord."

"I know that," Roland said.

"He will see reason."

Roland didn't answer. Justin stepped into the corridor and let the door fall shut behind him.

The hall was empty. Cold. The stone walls gave off a damp chill he could feel in his teeth, and somewhere deeper in the castle, morning prayer drifted from the chapel. Faint voices, steady and unhurried, as patient as old stone.

Blessed are the meek, for they shall inherit the earth.

Justin's jaw tightened. He thought of Whitethorne. Of thirty-seven people who had been meek, who had trusted that goodness and patience and the protection of a just king would be enough.

He thought of the shadow with wings that had passed over their rooftops in the dark, quiet and purposeful, while thirty-seven people slept.

His father had forbidden him from returning to Thornmoor. His father hadn't forbidden him from thinking.

And Justin knew, with clarity, that thinking was no longer enough.

In the deep passages beneath Thornmoor, the air changed before the light did.

Malric felt it first in his lungs, a heaviness that had nothing to do with depth, as though the mountain itself was breathing out something old and foul. The torches thinned here, guttered orange and dim, and by the time he reached the place where the stone changed color, the heat was pressing against his face like an open oven door. Smooth gray granite gave way to something darker, glassier, fused by ancient heat into surfaces that looked melted rather than carved. The walls had been shaped not by tools but by a body, something vast leaning against them century after century until the stone had learned to yield.

The guards stopped at the boundary. They always did. They

had learned what waited beyond it.

Malric kept walking.

He stripped his gauntlets slowly, deliberately, letting the leather fall into his hands, then tucked them into his belt. His bare palms registered the heat at once, a dry, pressing warmth rising from the stone beneath his boots, from the walls on either side, from somewhere below. The sulfur hit the back of his throat. Not a smell, exactly. More like a taste. Like something burned and never cooled.

Behind him, boots scraped stone.

The two soldiers dragged the prisoner around the final bend and into the chamber. An enemy scout taken past the northern pass, already interrogated, his information ex-tracted, his usefulness finished. His wrists were bound with rope worn thin from hours of struggling. His eyes found the fissure at the center of the chamber and went wide, pupils shrinking against instinct rather than light. The heat stole the sound from his throat before it could form words. He didn't beg. There was no air left in him for begging.

"Leave him," Malric said.

The soldiers turned and walked. Quickly. They did not run, because running would have meant acknowledging what they were leaving him with.

Malric stepped forward just far enough to cut the bindings with one stroke of his knife. The rope fell. The scout stum-bled, confusion pulling his face in two directions at once, and some animal part of him turned toward the fissure as though his legs had already understood what his mind refused. From the darkness below came a sound that was not quite breath, not quite wind. Slow. Immense. Lungs drawing in air that had not seen sunlight in centuries.

The floor vibrated under Malric's boots. Not a tremor. A rhythm. Almost like a heartbeat, if hearts could be the size of houses.

He stepped back to the place he had marked in his memory as safe. The boundary. The edge of the heat where darkness had never quite reached. He had found it through observation, the careful kind, conducted over years. He stood there now and waited with the patience of a man who understood patterns, who had mapped the creature's cycles of hunger and stillness with the same precision he applied to logistics and troop movements.

The darkness moved.

Not fully into the light, because it never came fully out. It never revealed itself entire. But something vast shifted at the edge of the fissure, and for one moment the faint glow caught a curve of scaled hide. Scales the size of shields. Black as obsidian and twice as hard. They vanished back into shadow before his eyes could measure what he'd seen, and the stone groaned beneath a weight that had no human equivalent.

The scout screamed once.

The sound went up through the passages, through the stone and the dark and the cold granite above, to where the guards stood at their posts. They heard it. They would say nothing. They would return to their stations and speak of other things. They had learned.

It ended quickly.

It always ended quickly. Efficiency was part of what this place was.

Heat rolled outward in a wave. Malric's eyes watered, his skin went slick with sweat, and then the wave subsided, drew back, settled into the low steady warmth that meant the creature was fed. For now. He waited until the chamber went still, until the only sounds were the soft crackle of heat against stone and the distant drip of water somewhere deeper in the mountain. Then he spoke into the dark.

"Eat," he said. His voice dropped straight into the fissure without echo, swallowed by the darkness as though the shadow itself had ears. "And remember who leaves you undisturbed. Who keeps the knights and their blessed steel out of these passages. Who ensures you can sleep and feed without interruption, so long as you serve the purposes that benefit us both."

No answer. There never was. Whatever intelligence lived in that ancient skull had either forgotten human language or simply found it beneath notice.

Only the low, steady breath. Rising and falling. Bending the torchlight in ways that had nothing to do with wind.

Malric replaced his gauntlets with the same deliberate care he'd used to remove them. He considered what he had built here. A weapon that required no forging, no supply lines, no treasury. Only a steady provision of prisoners, enemies, villagers from settlements remote enough to go uninvestigated, insignificant enough not to draw questions from Highstone. Above, the north would sleep more easily tonight because the raids had stopped, because the creature was fed and would not hunt. Rumors would move through the villages the way rumors always did, speaking of Thornmoor's power, of Lord Malric's mysterious reach, of enemies who vanished in the night. Fires blamed on accident. Shadows on imagination. And the truth staying buried here in the dark, where only he could reach it.

He turned toward the steps. His boots found them from memory as he climbed back toward the light, turning over what he had arranged. Justin's conflict with his father was the first fruit of what had been planted at Whitethorne. The village had been a calculated loss, a demonstration designed with precision, staged to expose the inadequacy of King Roland's patient justice and pull the young prince into Malric's orbit. If the raids continued, if more villages burned, if the king's authority looked increasingly helpless against threats that only Malric seemed equipped to contain, then the rest would follow. Power was not given by bloodline. It was seized by those willing to master what others feared to touch.

Behind him, in the deep dark where no oaths held and no banners meant anything, something shifted.

Scales rasped against stone. The sound of it was slow and enormous, like swords being drawn by the hundreds, like a mountain settling onto its own foundations.

Not obedience. Malric was already too far up the steps to feel the difference. But it was not obedience. It was hunger, the only thing in that creature that had survived the centuries intact, the only truth that time had not worn down. Hunger that could never be fully satisfied. Only briefly redirected. Only temporarily quieted.

Feeding a dragon does not make you its master.

It makes you its most convenient servant.

- **Chapter IX** -

The castle settled into silence after compline. Justin sat at the edge of his bed and listened to the quiet: footsteps somewhere down a distant corridor, the creak of timber finding its ease against the cold, and then, below, a door closing softly.

He did not light a candle. The moonlight through his window was sufficient.

He moved through the room carefully, choosing the heavy cloak, the one lined with wool that his father had given him two winters ago, and his riding gloves, and the leather satchel his mother had pressed into his hands three years back, still sturdy, still plain as the day she'd packed it for his first ride out. A second tunic, folded and placed inside. Bread wrapped in cloth from the evening meal he hadn't finished. A waterskin. A tinderbox.

He left the formal doublet on its peg. Left the book of Proverbs his father had set on his writing desk that morning. Left the silver clasp Lawrence had given him last spring, shaped like a hawk in flight, cast in silver, because some things were too heavy to carry.

His sword belt hung on the peg by the door. He stared at it.

The leather was worn smooth where his hand always gripped it. The buckle bore the mark of Highstone's forge, a small anvil stamped into the brass, and he knew every nick in that stamp, had noticed it a hundred times without meaning to.

He buckled it on. *This is not rebellion,* he told himself as he fastened the clasp.

He checked the blade in its sheath. Clean, sharp, ready.

This is clarity.

His father believed in patience. In virtue. In waiting for the right moment, the right answer, the right alignment of wisdom and conscience. But Whitethorne had waited, and thirty-seven people were gone. Justin pulled the strap tight and tested the sword's weight at his hip, finding it solid in a way that words and councils and prayers had stopped feeling weeks ago.

Malric had asked whether he was ready, and Justin didn't know the answer. He knew only that he could not stay here, forbidden and silent, while the mountains burned and his father prayed for guidance that never came, while villages disappeared and the council debated and the strange thing he'd seen in the Thornmoor chapel —

He stopped.

His reflection stared back from the darkened window glass, pale and lean. His father's eyes in a younger face. He looked away, slung the satchel over his shoulder, and moved to the door.

The corridor outside was dark and empty.

The castle at night was a different place. Justin had walked these halls a thousand times. Never like this. Never with the torches burned to low orange threads and the shadows sprawled long across the stone, never with his boots placed so carefully, his heartbeat so loud.

The air was cold, colder than it had any right to be even for autumn, and it carried old smoke and stone and the faint sweetness of beeswax drifting up from somewhere below.

He passed a window and slowed, looking out at the courtyard lying still beneath the stars. The well. The training yard. The stable where his horse waited, unsaddled, unaware. He'd have to wake the stableboy or saddle the horse himself in silence. The thought tightened his chest, but he kept walking.

The main stair curved down through the heart of the castle, its stone worn smooth in the center from generations of boots. His grandfather had walked these steps. His great-grandfather. Men who had ruled with wisdom and strength and the blessing of the crown. Men who had not doubted.

Justin descended slowly, one hand trailing along the wall. The stone was cold beneath his palm, solid and unchanging.

Halfway down, a faint sound reached him through a closed door — his father's chamber. Low, even, barely there. The murmur of a voice, too quiet to make out words but unmistakable in its cadence. Roland was praying. Justin's hand stilled against the stone wall. He stood there for one breath, then another, his throat tightening in a way he did not examine. He walked on.

He passed the chapel with its door closed and no light showing beneath it, and he thought of his father kneeling there in the mornings, head bowed and hands folded, the stillness around him like armor. Justin's steps slowed. Then he kept walking.

At the base of the stair, he crossed into the great hall.

The hearth had been banked for the night, but embers still glowed faintly in the ash, and the long tables were empty, the banners motionless overhead. Highstone's lion, mouth open in a silent roar.

In strength and mercy.

The house motto, embroidered beneath the lion in gold thread. Justin looked at it for a moment, then looked away.

At Thornmoor, the hall would have been full of men even at midnight. Guards at every door, patrols crossing the courtyard in shifts: efficiency, readiness, power that did not sleep. Here there was only warmth lingering in the stone long after the fire died, in the tapestries, in the way the moonlight fell through the high windows and lay quiet on the floor.

Justin pushed through the outer door and stepped into the courtyard.

The cold hit him full. His breath misted out ahead of him. His boots crunched softly over frost-rimmed cobblestones, and above him the sky stretched clear and vast, scattered with more stars than a man could count. He crossed to the gate slowly, the iron-banded weight of it familiar in the dark.

He had opened it a hundred times. A thousand. Never alone. Never in secret. Never without permission.

He stopped before it and set his hand on the latch. The metal was so cold it burned.

Beyond the gate, the northern road disappeared into darkness. He couldn't see the mountains from here, but he knew they were there, waiting, silent, full of things his father wouldn't name. Behind him, Highstone rose warm and solid against the night, torchlight flickering in a few high windows, the chapel bell tower standing dark against the stars, its cross a thin shadow against the sky.

Home.

Justin's hand tightened on the latch. He thought of Malric's voice in the Thornmoor courtyard, asking whether he was ready. Thought of the men in formation, the efficiency, the certainty.

Strength does not apologize.

He lifted the bar, and the iron scraped softly against the brackets before he stopped.

The memory came without warning.

His father, kneeling in the armory the morning before the ride to Graylor Pass. Three years ago, and Justin had gone looking for him and found him there alone, sword laid across his knees, head bowed.

The light was gray and early, the kind that came before the sun had fully committed to the day. Justin stood in the doorway and watched. Roland's face was still, not peaceful, because Justin had long since learned the difference, but still the way stone was still, the way deep water was. His lips moved and no sound came. His hands rested palms-down on the blade, as if he were holding something fragile, something that might break if he gripped it.

What are you praying for? Justin had wanted to ask. *Strength? Victory? Some kind of answer?*

He hadn't asked. When Roland finally rose, his face was composed. He saw Justin in the doorway, nodded once, lifted the sword, sheathed it, and walked past without a word.

Even then, standing in that gray armory light, Justin had understood he'd witnessed something he wasn't ready to understand.

Another memory. Elayne in the corridor, her face not angry but cold, disapproving in a way that was somehow worse than anger.

That is how one fights, Justin had said, and she'd looked at him as if she were seeing a stranger where she'd expected someone she knew.

I believe men are capable of more than survival, she said, quiet and level, and he hadn't answered. Hadn't known how.

When she turned to leave, her eyes held something that sat between grief and pity. Whether it was for him or for what she saw him becoming, he couldn't say. It was strange to carry a near-stranger's look that long. Strange that it had lodged in him the way it had.

But it had.

The chapel at Thornmoor.

Dust on the altar. The tapestry of the shepherd and the lamb hung crooked on the wall, slightly off-plumb, as if someone had straightened it once and then stopped caring. The candles were unlit, the altar cloth faded to a tired gray, and the air was stale with the smell of cold stone and old wax and nothing else. No incense. No fire. No breath of anyone who'd prayed there recently.

Justin had stood in the doorway and felt it: not evil, not darkness. Absence.

Malric's voice came from behind him, low and steady. *We do not pretend the mountains are tame.*

And Justin had realized, in that moment, that he agreed. His father did pretend, not with words but with patience, with waiting, with the quiet confidence that virtue and wisdom would eventually prove sufficient.

Whitethorne had proven they were not.

But staring at the dust and the crooked tapestry, Justin had felt a hollowness that was nothing like peace. He'd stood there a long time, and only one question had come: *What does it cost to stop pretending?*

He still didn't know.

The last memory hit him like a hand pressed flat against his chest.

The roar. Low, distant, rolling up through the cavern beneath Thornmoor like thunder that had never found the sky. Not wind. Not rockfall. Something else, something older, a sound that had no clean name.

Justin had been standing in the courtyard when it came. Around him, soldiers went still. Horses shifted, ears flat, whites showing at the edges of their eyes.

The sound moved through the ground, through the stone, through the soles of Justin's boots and up into his chest, where it settled like a second heartbeat. It hadn't been loud, that was what he remembered most, it hadn't been loud at all. But it was deep, deep enough to bypass the ears entirely, deep enough to feel ancient in a way that stone and bone both understood.

And then the sense that something knew he was there. Not with eyes. Not with thought. With recognition, the way a wolf recognizes prey, the way fire recognizes wood.

He'd stood frozen, his hand on his sword hilt, while the sound moved through him like a question spoken in a language he had no words for.

When it faded, the silence was worse.

The silence felt like waiting.

Justin's hand froze on the latch.

The gate was unbarred. The road lay open. All he had to do was push.

He stood in the cold, breath misting, heart loud in his ears. He thought of Malric's certainty, of the way his men moved without hesitation, without the weight of questions that circled and never landed. He thought of his father kneeling in silence and rising calm, of the sorrow in the face that had forbidden him to go back to Thornmoor. He thought of Whitethorne. Thirty-seven people who had trusted that goodness was a kind of armor.

And he thought of the roar, and the recognition, and the winged shadow the soldiers talked about in low voices and his father refused to name.

He couldn't say which of them was right.

The wind came across the courtyard, cold and sharp, pulling at his cloak, stinging the corners of his eyes. Far to the north, past the hills, past the edge of hearing, something rumbled. Thunder, maybe. Or stone shifting deep in the mountains. Or nothing at all.

His hand slipped from the latch.

He stood there a moment longer, looking at the gate, at the road beyond it, at the darkness that stretched north toward Thornmoor and the answers he thought he needed. His father kneeling with his palms flat on a sword. Elayne's eyes in the corridor. A crooked tapestry and cold, stale air. A roar that felt like recognition.

He couldn't make the pieces fit. Not into Malric's shape, not into his father's. The certainty he'd packed alongside the bread and the tinderbox, the anger that had felt so much like clarity, had dissolved the moment he tried to act on it.

Justin lowered the bar. The iron settled back into its brackets with a soft, final sound.

He turned and walked back across the courtyard, his boots crunching on frost, and he did not look behind him.

His chamber was exactly as he'd left it.

He set down the satchel and unbuckled the sword and placed them both on the floor beside the bed. He sat on the edge of the mattress. Moonlight slanted through the window. Somewhere below, a timber creaked, a door closed, and then the castle was quiet again.

He had not left. But he had not stayed because his father was right.

He'd stayed because the weight of not understanding was heavier than the weight of certainty, because doubt, when examined, was more honest than conviction.

Justin lay back and stared at the ceiling, thinking of the gate, and the road, and the choice he'd almost made. He thought of the roar in the darkness. Low. Distant. Patient.

He closed his eyes.

- **Chapter X** -

The letter came three days later. A royal courier carried it, and the gate captain brought it straight up to Malric's study without opening it, knowing better than to slow anything bearing the king's seal. Red wax. Roland's stag and crown, pressed deep.

Malric was at his desk when the captain entered. Maps lay spread before him: supply routes through the northern passes, timber yields from the foothills, grain stores calculated against the winter ahead. He finished the notation he'd been writing before he set down his pen.

"My lord," the captain said. "From Highstone."

Malric took the letter. He turned it over, studied the seal, then broke it with his thumb. The captain stood still while Malric read. His eyes moved across the page, face giving nothing away. When he finished, he folded the letter once and laid it beside the maps.

"That will be all," he said.

The captain shifted his weight. "My lord, if there is a re-ply—"

"There is not."

The captain bowed and pulled the door shut behind him, softly.

Malric sat alone. Wind moved through the courtyard outside, and somewhere below, a hammer rang against an anvil, steady, measured, unhurried. He picked up the letter again and read it through.

Duke Malric,

I write to inform you that Prince Justin will no longer travel to Thornmoor for instruction. His duties at Highstone require his full attention, and I have determined that his education is best continued here, under my direct supervision.

I thank you for the time you have given to his training. It has been noted.

May the Lord grant you wisdom in your service to the realm.

Roland, King of Meridia

Malric set the letter down and leaned back in his chair. His gaze returned to the maps, to the careful lines marking borders and roads, the small notations in his own hand: villages, populations, resources. Everything reduced to what it was.

Roland had made his choice. The boy was back at Highstone, back inside walls built on ideals and prayers and the belief that patience could hold a border, that mercy was a form of governance, that waiting for men to choose virtue would somehow protect them from what pressed down out of the mountains.

A faint smile touched Malric's mouth.

"He will return," he said quietly.

The study was empty. No one heard him. But Malric didn't say it as hope. He said it as fact, the way a man states a calculation he's already confirmed. The boy had seen what authority looked like. He'd stood in a courtyard where two hundred men moved as one, where discipline replaced doubt. That kind of thing didn't leave a person.

Justin would remember. And when Roland's mercy failed, when the villages burned and the people cried out for protection their king could not give — the boy would come back.

Malric rose and walked to the window. Beyond the courtyard, the mountains stood dark against the sky, and smoke drifted from the northern peaks, thin and pale in the afternoon light.

He watched it for a long moment, then turned and left the study.

The descent began in the chapel.

Malric pushed the door open and stepped inside. Dust on the altar. The tapestry of the shepherd and the lamb still hung crooked on the far wall, its colors faded to gray. The candles in their iron stands had not been lit in months, and the air smelled of cold wax and stone and nothing else. No one came here. No one had reason to.

He crossed to the altar and gripped its edge. The stone was heavy, but it moved on hidden runners, grinding softly as it slid aside to reveal a narrow stairway cut into the floor.

Dark air rose from below, warm and stale.

Malric descended without hesitation.

The passage beyond was older than the castle above. Much older. The walls were rough-cut stone, blackened in places by heat that had soaked into the rock over centuries. Sulfur hit him first, faint, then stronger with each step. Iron brackets held torches whose flames burned steady and low, as though the air itself resisted them.

The passage sloped downward. The stone beneath his boots was smooth, worn smooth by generations of Thornmoor lords who had walked this path before him. His grandfather. His father. Each had descended into the mountain's heart, and each had returned carrying the same knowledge.

The cold of the castle gave way to warmth. Then to heat that pressed against his skin, dense and close. He loosened his collar but didn't slow.

The passage turned and narrowed. The ceiling dropped until he had to duck beneath an outcropping of stone. The torches grew fewer. The darkness between them thickened, heavy with something that had nothing to do with the absence of light.

His footsteps echoed off the walls, sharp and rhythmic and solitary. Somewhere far below, water dripped in slow intervals, each drop carrying through the stone with the patience of something that had been falling for a very long time. Deeper still came the rumble. Not loud. Not close. Just present, the way a held breath is present, felt in the chest before it's heard.

Then the passage opened, and Malric stopped.

The cavern was vast.

The ceiling vanished into shadow so complete that no torch-light reached it. The walls curved away into darkness, their surfaces slick with moisture, streaked with mineral deposits that caught the dim light: copper, iron, and something else that shimmered like old gold. The floor was broken by fissures, their edges glowing red, heat rising from them in slow waves. The smell was sulfur and ash and something underneath both, something older, something with no name.

Malric stood at the cavern's edge.

He didn't call out. He waited.

The air shifted.

Not wind, for there was no wind this deep. It was breath. Ancient, deliberate, slow.

The fissures brightened. The shadows around him stretched and trembled. The dripping water stopped. The rumble moved upward through the stone until it filled the cavern, rolling through the walls and the floor and the bones of the mountain itself.

In the darkness at the far end of the cavern, something moved.

Not a shape. Not yet. The absence of light, a shadow within shadow, massive beyond comprehension, utterly still in its enormity.

Malric's heart beat steady. He'd been here before. He knew what waited in the dark.

The movement stopped.

Silence.

Sweat gathered at his temples. Heat pressed against him on all sides, thick and suffocating, the air tasting of iron and fire. He planted his feet and kept his hands loose at his sides.

He didn't step back.

Then, slowly, impossibly slowly, a single eye opened.

It was golden.

Not the gold of coins or crowns. Not the gold of firelight or any sunset. The gold of molten metal, of fire compressed into form and held there. It didn't blink. It didn't move. It simply was, fixed and unreadable and utterly sovereign.

The eye found Malric.

The weight of that gaze settled on him like a stone placed on his chest. His breath went shallow. His hands tightened into fists.

He didn't flinch.

"You serve Meridia's future," Malric said.

His voice was steady. Calm. The voice of a man who had come to this place many times, who had spoken these words into this darkness, who had stood in the heat and the weight of that gaze and walked back up the passage certain of what he'd left behind.

The dragon was a tool. A weapon. The apex force of the mountains, yes, but a force that could be directed. His ancestors had done exactly that. They had built Thornmoor on this alliance, had held the eastern mountains of Meridia because the dragon's presence alone kept enemies at the borders.

Malric believed this.

He had to.

The eye didn't close. Didn't shift.

Nothing happened.

The fissures pulsed, slow and rhythmic, like a heartbeat buried deep in the stone. Sweat ran down the back of Malric's neck. His tunic clung to him.

Then the dragon exhaled.

Not a roar. Not a growl. Just breath.

It rolled across the cavern like a wave and hit Malric full in the face, heat so dense it had texture, weight, a pressure his lungs pushed against. The stone beneath his boots went warm, then hot. The fissures flared. Red light flooded the walls, the scales of the dragon still hidden in the darkness but visible now in fragments, enormous and scarred and old beyond reckoning.

Malric's jaw locked. His hands shook. He drove his knees

straight and kept himself upright.

He didn't step back.

The exhale continued, longer and hotter, until the air itself felt like something burning. His vision blurred at the edges. His lungs ached.

The golden eye watched.

Not with malice.

Not with anger.

With nothing.

The exhale faded. The heat pulled back. The glow from the fissures dimmed.

The golden eye stayed open.

Malric stood in the silence, breathing hard, fighting to slow it. He'd come here many times. Each time he'd spoken into the dark, felt the gaze, endured the heat, and left believing the same thing.

The dragon understood. It served. When the time came, it would act.

He'd mastered what no king in three generations had dared approach. The dragon had not attacked him. Had not refused him. It had listened, and in that listening, Malric found what he needed.

He turned and walked back toward the passage.

Behind him, the eye didn't close.

The darkness didn't move.

But something in the cavern shifted, not in the stone, not in the air, but in the silence itself. A presence, patient and sovereign, waiting for nothing and no one.

Malric climbed the passage without looking back. The heat faded step by step. The sulfur thinned. The torches burned brighter, their flames steady and familiar. His breathing eased.

By the time he reached the chapel, his face had settled back into its mask.

He slid the altar back into place. The stone settled with a low grinding sound, and the stairway disappeared beneath it as though it had never been there. He walked out through the chapel door and into the castle's empty corridors. No one saw him. No one asked.

Roland's letter was still on the desk where he'd left it.

Malric glanced at it once, then turned to the maps, picked up his pen, and made a small notation beside one of the northern villages. A calculation. A projection.

The dragon would act when the time came. It always had. His ancestors had proven as much. The alliance was old, tested, and true.

Malric believed this.

He had to.

Far below, in the cavern beneath Thornmoor, the golden eye remained open.

The darkness breathed, slow and deep and patient.

Something stirred in the shadows. Not movement. Not yet. Just the weight of it, something vast coiled in the stone, pressing against the edges of itself.

Not for Malric. Not for Meridia. For nothing but its own appetite.

The fissures glowed. The mountain held its secrets.

And in the dark, the dragon did not sleep.

The End

- Discussion Questions -

Prince Justin struggles between two very different visions of leadership — one based on control and fear, and one based on justice and mercy. Which do you think is harder to live by? Why?

King Roland believes strength and mercy can exist together. Do you agree? Can someone be strong without becoming harsh? Give examples from the story or real life.

At several moments, Justin must choose whether to act out of fear or faith. Why do you think fear can be so powerful? What helps someone choose courage instead?

The Black Duke represents a very clear and decisive kind of power. Why might that kind of leadership be appealing to people during uncertain times? What are the dangers of it?

By the end of the book, how has Justin changed? What kind of king do you think he is becoming? What challenges do you think he will face next?

Acknowledgments

My sincere thanks to my sister, Lorraine, and my brother-in-law, Jason, whose careful reading and thoughtful editorial notes strengthened this manuscript in its earliest stages.

To my wife, Rachel—thank you for your constant support, patience, and encouragement throughout the writing of this book and my creative projects.

To my children, who are daily reminders of why stories matter, and why legacy is worth building.

I am grateful to my entire family for their unwavering support, and to the loyal readers who continue to invest their time and trust in these pages.

About the Author

R.C. Jameson writes stories shaped by history, faith, and the enduring tension between power and virtue. His work explores questions of leadership, loyalty, and legacy in worlds both distant and familiar.

Prince Justin and the Black Duke of Thornmoor is the first installment in an unfolding saga.

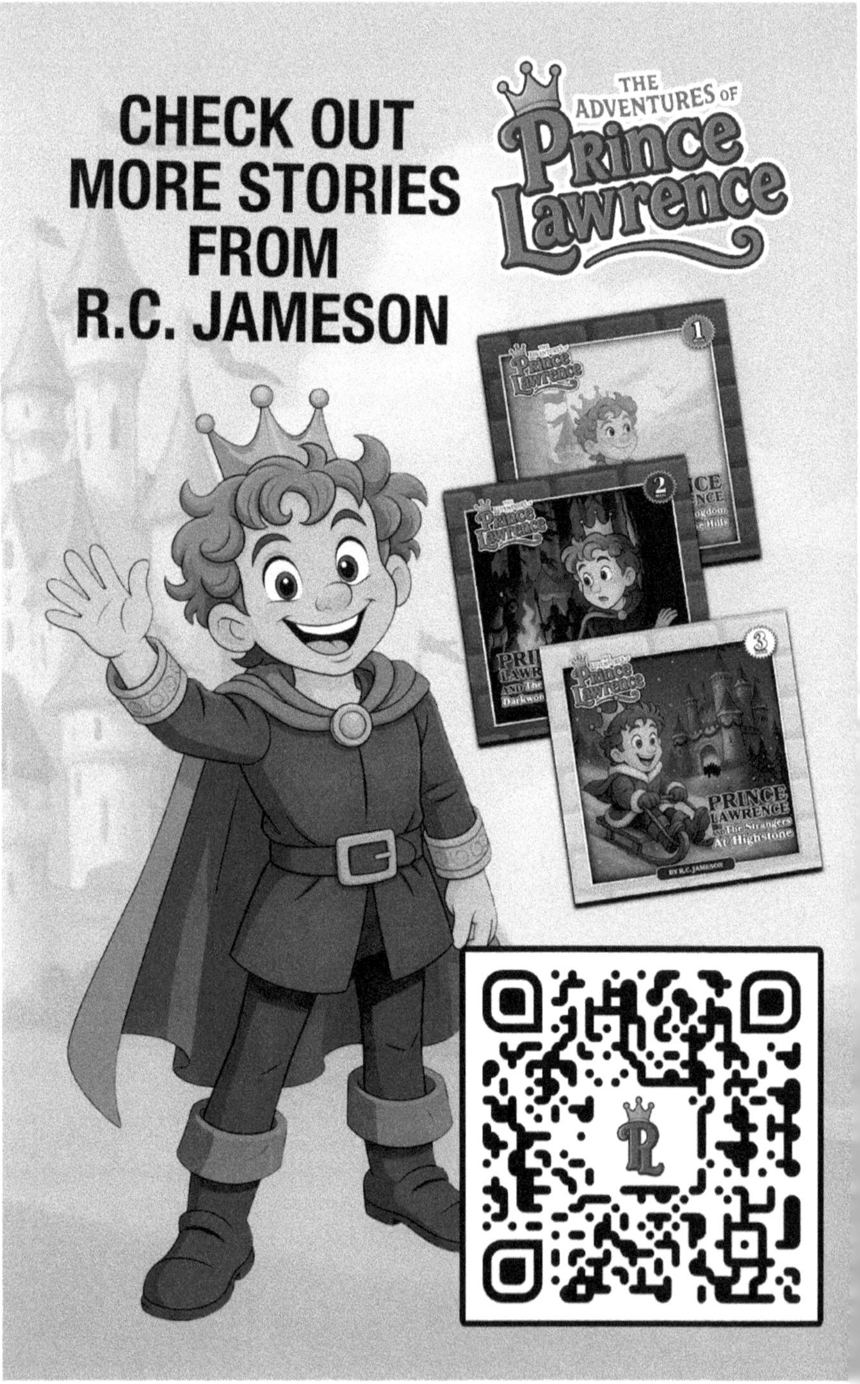

CHECK OUT MORE STORIES FROM R.C. JAMESON

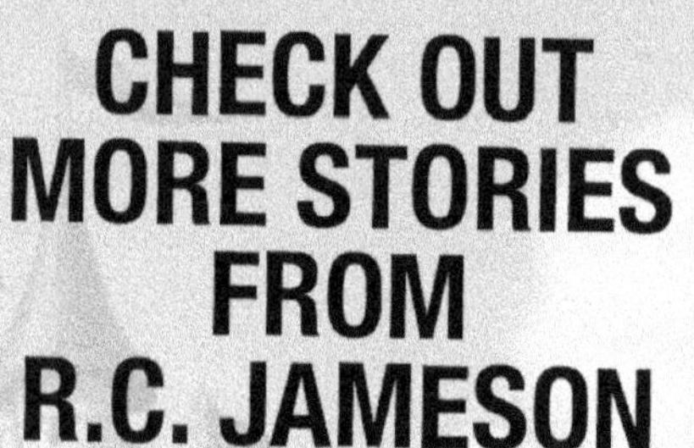